HER CHRISTMAS DUKE: A REGENCY ROMANCE

CHRISTMAS KISSES (BOOK 3)

ROSE PEARSON

HER CHRISTMAS DUKE

Thus far, the summer Season had gone just as Augusta had expected. She had enjoyed a good many occasions, stepped out to dance with various gentlemen, and had made a few new acquaintances – one of whom immediately came to join her the moment she stepped into the ballroom.

"Good evening, Lady Augusta!" Miss Keen, her eyes bright with obvious excitement, came hurrying towards her. "I am so very glad to see you here. I have been looking for someone to stand with and thus far, none of my other acquaintances have shown themselves!"

Augusta smiled softly. Miss Keen was something of a wallflower with a very quiet nature and a tendency to shy away from certain things unless she was in company – large crowds being one such thing. As far as Augusta knew, Miss Keen did not have many friends and thus, she was very glad to slip her arm through Miss Keen's and walk a little further into the room.

"Is your mother nearby?"

"Yes, but she is taken up with my sister, of course." Miss

Keen laughed and rolled her eyes. "Although now she is engaged, I must hope my mother fawns over me in much the same way, for I should very much like to make a match this Season! Mother has stated she will return to London for the little Season, however, if both of her daughters are not wed by the time the summer Season ends, so there is still hope!" She laughed again. "I believe my father wishes us both to be taken off his hands by the year's end."

"Not that we should complain about such a thing if we are to make *good* matches." Augusta smiled as Miss Keen nodded fervently. "I confess, while there have been many gentlemen who have greeted me thus far and many who have been cordial, I have not yet found anyone of whom I would particularly take note of."

"No?" Miss Keen's eyes widened. "Goodness, I confess I have set my eyes on a good many gentlemen, considering that any of them would be a suitable match for me! Not that any of them have looked at me in return, however."

Augusta settled one hand on her friend's arm. "I am sure one of them will, in time." Lifting one shoulder, she threw a broad smile to her friend. "I find myself in much the same situation, for no gentleman has expressed an interest in taking me for a short walk around Hyde Park or has asked me for a carriage ride."

"Not as yet, anyway."

"Precisely." Smiling encouragingly, Augusta tapped Miss Keen's hand before dropping her own. "That must be the attitude we adorn ourselves with – the right gentleman has not found us as yet but shall reveal himself in time."

Miss Keen caught her breath, one hand going to her heart, her eyes wide and fixed on something – or someone – across the room. A little confused, Augusta considered for a moment whether she had said something untoward, only to look in the very same direction as Miss Keen. Her own breath hitched, but she quickly turned her gaze away, pushing away the flicker of excitement which had caught her. How many times had she to remind herself that the Duke of Meyrick was nothing more than an ordinary gentleman? Yes, he bore a title which was only a little lower than the King himself, but to her mind, that meant very little as regarded his character. From what she had seen thus far, the loftier the title, the more inclined the gentleman was to be arrogant, overly confident and perhaps even a little roguish. No doubt, August told herself, it would be the same with the Duke of Meyrick himself.

"I think the Duke of Meyrick is the most handsome gentleman in all of London – if not in all of England!"

Augusta looked over at her friend, catching the soft sigh that came as Miss Keen watched the Duke cross the ballroom, coming closer to them both. Her own lips twisted.

"Yes, I quite agree. He is the most handsome, most amiable, most genteel and the most generous of gentlemen in all of society." Her friend rolled her eyes at Augusta's droll tone. "All the things which are expected of a Duke, I suppose. How fortunate we are to have him here in London during the summer Season!" Augusta did nothing to hide the heaviness from her tone, fully aware her friend was looking rather displeased over her jesting.

"You need not make your lack of interest so *entirely* obvious," Miss Keen took a deep breath and then let out yet another wistful sigh as Augusta looked in the Duke's direction. He was, at present, throwing his head back and laughing at something another gentleman had said – and there were at least three young ladies fixed in their attentions, their eyes a little glassy as they gazed at him. Yes, she considered, he was just as she had expected: confident, delighting in the attentions of others and, no doubt, somewhat brash with it.

"I think him *terribly* handsome. I do wish he would pay even the smallest of attention to me." Another dramatic sigh followed, leaving Augusta somewhat surprised. Was her friend truly this overcome simply by the nearness of the Duke of Meyrick? She did not even *know* the gentleman – nor his character! Surely one should not be so affected by a gentleman simply because of his title.

"Do you think he knows how much the people in London admire him?" Miss Keen raised a questioning glance towards Augusta, who quickly pushed her surprised expression away, her lips curving into a laughing smile.

"I think you speak of the young ladies of London, surely? I think mayhap, gentlemen admire him also but certainly, is it the *ladies* who appear to dote on him – both young and old alike! There will be young ladies who seek his company in the hope of catching his eye and, should their hopes be fulfilled, his bride – and their mothers equally think on him in the hope of such a thing for their daughters!" Her smile grew. "Yes, my dear friend. I am very sure the Duke of Meyrick knows how much he is admired. It would be unexpected if it were not to be so, for even if he was to be the most unhandsome fellow, I think almost every young unmarried lady would still desire to be in his company. It is the way of things with Dukes, is it not?"

She said this without malice, meaning only that the Duke of Meyrick was so highly titled and wealthy, it was impossible for him to be ignored by even the most disinclined member of the *ton* – including herself. She was aware of the Duke of Meyrick's presence whenever she stepped into the same room as he, aware of where he stood and what he was doing, but she never permitted herself to be interested in him in any way. Certainly she had to remind herself he was not any more or less worthy of her time and consideration than others, recalling that a title did not make a gentleman worthy of her notice! This time, however, Augusta allowed her gaze to linger on the gentleman for a moment, silently wondering whether or not such standing could ever be a burden. Did he find the *ton*'s notice weighty? Was it ever a heavy responsibility around his neck? Or did he find himself delighting in it?

The Duke of Meyrick was still laughing at something which had been said during the conversation and Augusta had to silently admit to herself he was a handsome fellow. As he flung his head back in another guffaw, the light sent a copper tint through his hair, his grin pouring brightness into his features. Augusta tilted her head, thinking silently the Duke did appear to be a strong gentleman, given his broad shoulders, height and even in the way he carried himself giving such an impression – although she feared he might crush her hand in his grip, should he ever dance with her!

Miss Keen turned towards her, interrupting her quiet thoughts. "I assume you have been introduced to him?"

Augusta nodded. "Yes, I have. I do not think he took any particular interest in me, however. I am one of *many* young ladies he has been introduced to this Season." She grinned back at her friend who merely shook her head again at Augusta's obvious disinclination towards the Duke of Meyrick. "You need not think I am in any way upset by his lack of interest. Quite the opposite, in fact."

"Quite the opposite?" Miss Keen blinked, her smile dying away as she searched Augusta's face. "Whatever do you mean by saying such a thing?"

Augusta lifted one shoulder. "Simply to say, I have no concern over his indifference. I am not upset he does not look upon me with great favor. I do not sit alone at night and weep over his lack of interest in my company. My dreams have not been dashed, for I never once allowed myself to consider or dream that I should be the wife of a Duke." Seeing her friend's eyes widen a little- as though every young lady ought to allow herself such a dream at one point or another, Augusta laughed merrily. "I think with great practicality, my dear friend. I am the daughter of Viscount Sutton. What could a young woman such as myself expect? A decent match, certainly, but never a match with a Duke!"

Miss Keen shook her head, her hand going to Augusta's arm. "One can never tell," she responded sagely, as if she were filled with some great wisdom and had experience in the art of creating a suitable match between a gentleman and a lady. "What you have never allowed yourself to dream of may, in fact, be exactly what takes place."

Augusta could not help but chuckle at the very idea, thinking it nothing more than a jest. "On rare occasions, I am certain matches are made for others when there is such a difference in social standing but I highly doubt it would be so for me." Her shrug came a second time as she spread her hands. "I am quite certain the Duke of Meyrick will marry the daughter of another Duke, or perhaps a Marquess. A match of that sort would be the most sensible and expected arrangement, would it not? Besides," she continued hastily, before her friend could interrupt. "I have no interest in the Duke of Meyrick. I can assure you. My words are quite true."

Miss Keen's fingers suddenly dug into Augusta's arm. "You must silence yourself this instant, for I believe the Duke of Meyrick is coming towards us! I do not know why he has sought to consider us, but we must be ready for his attentions!"

Sighing inwardly at her friend's fierce reaction. Augusta allowed herself a brief glance in the Duke of Meyrick's direction. He was, in fact, coming close to them, but his presence gave Augusta very little concern. Whether he came to speak with them or not, she did not particularly mind, although, evidently, Miss Keen found his approaching presence overwhelming, given how she gasped.

"You must smile; we must look as though we are talking of something!" Her friend's tone was hurried, her anxiety obvious. "Come, say something which will make me laugh. I look my best when I am smiling and I am certain I must appear rather terrified at present!"

It was Augusta who found herself laughing rather than Miss Keen, however, such was her mirth at her friend's request and the clear upset in her features. The Duke of Meyrick's face lit with a polite smile as he drew near, as Augusta managed to control her laughter just in time for his approach.

"And what is it two such beautiful ladies are smiling about, if I might be so bold as to ask?"

Glancing towards her friend, Augusta took in Miss Keen's slightly widened eyes, the flush to her cheeks, and the way her mouth had now formed a gentle circle. Sighing gently, she looked back to the Duke, meaning to answer him and wondering whether or not Miss Keen would ever be able to speak in front of him. Why anyone behaved in such a way around the Duke of Meyrick, she simply could not understand. He was only a gentleman – a highly titled one, yes, but only another one of the many titled gentlemen here in London – to her eyes at least, he held no refining interest.

"It is very bold of you to ask what secrets we ladies are sharing, Your Grace," she murmured quietly, all too aware of the gasp falling from Miss Keen's lips at her remark.

"Therefore, let us speak of the ball and other such things. Are you having a pleasant evening thus far?"

"So you will not tell me your secrets, then." The Duke did not seem to know whether to smile or to frown; his expression caught somewhere in between. "How very interesting. I confess I am all the more intrigued now! You cannot keep it from me."

"We were speaking of nothing of any great importance, Your Grace." Miss Keen's response came out in a tangled heap, her breath catching within between every word or two. "This ball is quite wonderful, is it not? I see you have danced almost every dance thus far.... I do not mean I have been continually watching you, however."

The Duke glanced at her, then looked to Augusta again, a frown catching his forehead. "Yes, and it has been a little fatiguing!" A smile began to grow, his lips quirking. "I am glad now to have stepped away for a time. It gives me opportunity to enjoy our conversation!"

"Unless you are promised to dance with a young lady," Augusta responded quickly. "We should not want you to step away from your obligations for our sake."

The smile which flickered across the Duke's lips immediately began to diminish. "I have no partner for the country dance, Miss Moir – and it is one of my favorite dances, too." His eyebrow lifted in gentle question, a spark now in his eye and a broad grin pushing at his lips and Augusta looked away sharply, suddenly concerned her questions were being taken in quite the opposite way as to what she desired. Was the Duke now wondering whether or not she herself wished to dance with him?

She looked to Miss Keen, hoping her friend would say something, finding herself recoiling from the Duke a little. She did not know precisely what it was but, at present, there was something about the Duke's smile she disliked. Mayhap it was the hint of arrogance she saw there or the silent expectation she would be more than willing to stand up with him. Eager to quickly turn such expectations on its head, she gestured to Miss Keen, speaking quickly now.

"I am certain my friend, Miss Keen, would be more than willing to stand up with you for the country dance, Your Grace. I myself find I am a little... fatigued at present."

Again came the swift intake of breath from her friend, but Augusta kept her gaze fixed on the Duke, smiling inwardly when his smile faltered. He could not refuse, of course, having given the distinct impression he was rather keen to dance and was not already engaged. After a few moments, he turned directly towards Miss Keen, who let out a squeak of either excitement or fear.

"Miss Keen." Inclining his head, he threw a quick glance towards Augusta. "The country dance, then?"

Miss Keen could do nothing but accept, her hand trembling a little as she took the Duke's outstretched one. Augusta watched with satisfaction as the Duke of Meyrick and Miss Keen stepped away. Her friend would be overwhelmed with delight now she was to dance with the Duke, whilst Augusta herself would no longer have to linger in the Duke's presence. This appeared to be a satisfactory conclusion for them all.

"My dear." Her mother, Lady Sutton, grasped at Augusta's hand as she came to stand directly in front of her. "I have news!" With her voice a little higher than usual and bright, flashing eyes that were seemingly filled with excitement, Augusta gave her mother her full attention.

"Yes, Mama?"

"I do not know if you will be able to believe this, but we

have *all* been invited to the Duke of Meyrick's Christmas house party!"

There was a breath of silence.

"The Duke of Meyrick's Christmas house party," Augusta repeated, her sense of satisfaction slowly beginning to wind away. "It is only the summer season. Whatever is there talk about Christmas for?"

"Because it is the Duke of Meyrick," her mother repeated, as though his name should be enough to explain. "Such invitations will be eagerly sought after and to have been given one so early is a great distinction."

"I see." Augusta took a few moments to interpret this news, realizing she was now to be in the Duke's company for the Christmas Season – a gentleman who she had clearly spurned only a few moments ago. Might it not be a little awkward? She caught the bottom of her lip between her teeth. No, surely it would not be, for the Duke of Meyrick would not remember her nor what she had just done in pushing Miss Keen forward in her place. As she had said to her friend only a few moments ago, the Duke was surrounded by adoring young ladies – it was very unlikely he would remember her!

"I should say, the invitation is from his mother, Lady Meyrick." Lady Sutton smiled brightly, as though it does not matter who the invitation had come from but Augusta immediately frowned.

"Does that mean, then, the Duke of Meyrick himself is not aware of the invitation?" Her eyes narrowed a little as her mother's eyes darted away.

"Is he aware of the house party, at least?"

Lady Sutton cleared her throat, still refusing to linger on Augusta's gaze "It does not matter whether or not the

Duke is aware of it as yet. He will be very pleased to have such excellent company in the winter, I am sure."

Augusta took a breath and let it out slowly, looking over her mother's shoulder to where the Duke of Meyrick was dancing with Miss Keen. "I do not think any gentleman would be overly delighted to learn of such plans only once they are all in place!"

"Regardless of what you think, my dear, we *are* to attend."

Taking her gaze directly back to her mother, Augusta's lips twisted for a moment at the gleam in her mother's eye. "I do hope you have no intentions of pushing me towards the Duke. I am disinclined towards drawing near to any gentleman of high title, simply because of his high position in society – and besides which, I am only the daughter of a Viscount and –"

Her mother squeezed her hand. "Such things have happened before," she proclaimed, her head turning as her eyes went to someone else. "Now, do stay where I can see you, but I must speak with Lady Colton and tell her of our amazing news. I think this house party shall be the talk of London by the morning!"

Before Augusta could protest, her mother had stepped away, leaving Augusta to stand alone. Closing her eyes for a moment, she folded her arms across her chest, her head tilted a little.

I do not want to be pushed towards the Duke of Meyrick.

With a sigh, she opened her eyes and continued to study the gentleman as he danced, finding no quickening of her heart nor excitement rising within her at the thought of attending his house party. Regardless of whether her own mother had intentions for her, there was certainly no desire to further her acquaintance with the Duke. There was a gentle pride which came with his distinction of rank, although she certainly did not hold such things against him, given he was always to be admired, always to be respected and always to be spoken well of. It did not engage her heart, did not draw her closer to him – and this house party did not fill her with even a modicum of excitement.

Her lips lifted in a small, slightly rueful smile, wondering what Miss Keen would say when such news was told her. No doubt her friend would be distinctly envious and, after a few moments' consideration, Augusta concluded it would be best not to tell her friend such news.

Taking in a deep breath, she let out a sigh, her hands dropping to her side. The last thing she had ever expected was to be invited to the Duke's residence, but it seemed now, in a few short months, she would be spending a great deal of time in his company... whether she wished to or not.

CHAPTER ONE

"You are aware I did not want this house party in the first place?"

Lady Meyrick lifted her chin. "My son, you have made your feelings quite clear." Her eyes flashed as Edward rolled his in a most obvious manner. "But I *had* hoped you would decide to be jovial regardless. In fact, I hoped you would find it very pleasing once it began."

Edward threw up his hands. "Mother, you made the arrangements before even *consulting* me as regarded my feelings. This was not what I had envisaged for the winter. I had thought to busy myself with a good many things."

"A good many things which could easily wait a month or two," his mother protested, holding her arms across her chest and narrowing her eyes into what was a very sharp expression. "Are you truly complaining to me now? Now when you have a house full of excellent company? Such an attitude is quite ridiculous... especially when you have so many people *eager* for your company."

Edward let out a slow breath, his stomach tightening. "Understand this, Mother, if your intentions for this house party are to encourage me in the direction of a particular lady, and I can assure you, your efforts will be in vain. I have absolutely no thought of matrimony at the present time, regardless of how much you might wish it for me."

His mother said nothing but her gaze grew all the more fixed. Silently, Edward wondered whether he had, in fact, guessed correctly for he could not tell from his mother's expression. Even from childhood, he had never been able to know what she was thinking, for Lady Meyrick had managed to perfect the art of keeping her features composed, regardless of whatever was going on inside. Dropping his hands, he flung them out either side for a moment.

"If you *have,* however, organized it all simply so I might enjoy myself, then I suppose I should be grateful to you for your endeavors."

"You suppose?" His mother shook her head. "Perhaps you might consider just how much of an effort I have put into making certain that our winter months are not filled with dreariness, *then,* mayhap, your gratitude might come a little more easily."

Guilt plunged itself into Edward' heart and he dropped his head, blowing out air in a frustrated sigh. "I am grateful for your efforts, Mother, of course. I would have preferred it, however, if you would have spoken with me at the very first inkling of such an idea so it could have been discussed."

"But you would have said no."

Edward frowned, no response coming to him. His mother was correct for, had she given him this suggestion, then there was very little doubt in his mind he would have pointedly refused. He might have considered having one or two friends and companions, but certainly not so many well connected families... or their eligible daughters.

"Very well, I shall accept such a thing from you." Heaving a sigh, he shook his head and looked away. "I have behaved well thus far, have I not? I may not be as eager as you might wish but I am sure our guests do not notice it."

"Except to those whom you have told." Lady Meyrick sniffed and looked away. "I have heard of your words to some particular friends, stating the house party was more my idea than yours. If you wish to have the guests believe you are happy for their presence, then you will have to put in a good deal more effort. Every guest here wants to see that you are enjoying this house party as much as they are."

Edward' jaw tightened but he chose to remain silent, waiting for his mother to continue and suspicious of what it was she was about to say.

"Speak with them, laugh with them. You have taken part in the parlor games, yes, but permit yourself to be a little less reserved." One shoulder lifted as she turned her head away from him. "Find those who are a little less integrated with the group and encourage them. You might consider speaking to Miss Williams a little more, for example."

"I knew it." Glaring at his mother, Edward stuck one finger towards her. She can get a little. "You do have particular intentions as regards to young ladies at this house party, do you not?"

"You seem to think so." The slight edge of nervousness to her voice made Edward close his eyes in frustration. To his mind, it was more than obvious his mother had every intention of encouraging a match between himself and one of the young ladies present. No doubt it was why so many of them had been invited! Rubbing one hand over his face, he shook his head and looked towards his mother again.

"You told me there was no intention for this house party

other than for it to bring a little brightness, a little entertainment and joy to our winter."

"And so it is!" Lady Meyrick protested, rising from her chair. "And if you should meet an amiable young lady, if you should seek to know her a little better, then what trouble will that be? It will be no trouble at all. In fact, it will be very pleasant indeed."

"And mayhap I will not," Edward stressed, throwing back a response immediately. "I do not require your help with this. If I want to find a bride, I am very well able to do so myself." A curl of temper began to light a fire in him, sending billowing smoke up towards his heart. "I have asked you time and again, over as many years as I can remember to remain out of my personal affairs."

Lady Meyrick lifted her chin, her hands going to her waist. "I would see you take such a responsibility seriously!" she countered, pouring oil onto an already furious fire. "You ought to be considering your future. You know I have no other son. If the worst should happen – and I do not like so much as thinking about it – but there is no succession! You have held the title for nearly six years and in all that time you have shown not even the smallest interest in taking a bride."

Clenching his hands, Edward struggled to keep the temper from his voice. "I have had a good many other responsibilities, Mother." Shooting his words back at her, he fought to keep his voice steady. "Now I am all the more disinclined towards the house party. Perhaps I shall speak only to married ladies, for that way I can give not even the *hint* of an impression to any of the other young ladies you have invited here."

His mother shook her head, her hands now clasped

tightly in front of her. "You would be foolish to behave so, as well you know."

Grimacing, Edward turned on his heel and made his way to the door, resisting the urge to stamp his feet like a petulant child. Flinging the door open, he stepped out into the hallway and marched along it, his hands still tight with irritation.

"I will not be pushed towards anyone." Muttering darkly to himself, he made his way towards his study, fully determined he would not give any obvious attention to Miss Williams, or to Miss Moir, or to *any* of the other young ladies who were present. If his mother's intention was to help him think about courting one of them, then she would be sorely disappointed. This was not why he had eventually agreed to the house party. These weeks were merely to enjoy himself, to bring a little light to an otherwise dark winter. It was certainly not to find himself interested in any of the young ladies here.

Slowing his steps as he arrived at the front of the house, Edward took in a deep breath and thought to step outside for a moment. The cool air might bring a little more calmness to him and thus, he made his way directly to the front door, yanking it open hard before stepping outside into the cold afternoon air. He had no more than taken a breath when something hard and cold slammed into one side of his face. Staggering back towards the door, he wiped blindly at his eyes, water beginning to run past his collar.

"Your Grace! I am so sorry." A loud exclamation drew near to him just as his cheek began to burn, his vision a little blurred. Blinking rapidly, he dug quickly into his pocket for his handkerchief, using it to wipe his face.

"I thought you were Lord Forrester," the voice continued. "Please, allow me."

A hand touched his, taking his handkerchief from him. Delicate fingers wiped first at one eye and then the other, before dabbing lightly at his cheek. It took a few moments still for Edward to regain his full vision, but when he did, his gaze took in the pale face of Miss Moir, his handkerchief still clutched in one hand. Her eyes were wide, her lips pulled back in a grimace, and lines drawn over her forehead which spoke of worry.

"A snowball fight?" Snorting, he looked away. "It is a little juvenile, is it not?"

The sharpness in his voice was more than he had intended, but his only response to his present embarrassment, it seemed, was to question the lady over what she was doing. It was not the best of responses, he knew, but given the circumstances, it was all he could say.

"I suppose it is." Miss Moir looked away. "Nonetheless, there are a few of us playing a game together and even if it is a little juvenile, you are welcome to join us... especially since you are a little damp already." A brightness came into her voice, her eyes lighting a little as the worry ran from her expression – but Edward only drew himself up, his frame tight. First of all, he had been forced to endure his mother pretending she had no intention of pushing any young lady to him and now, he had been hit furiously in the face by a snowball meant for Lord Forrester. His frustration, he did not think, could get any bigger without exploding into fury and thus, he shook his head.

"I do not think Dukes plays such games as this."

The slight curl of his lip immediately elicited a response in Miss Moir, for her cheeks suddenly flared. She did not appear to be embarrassed however, for her gaze did not drop from his. Instead, her hands went to her hips and her eyes narrowed a little as she tilted her head a little.

"Then you will miss out on a great deal of joviality, Your Grace." Her eyebrow arched. "There is nothing childish about enjoying a winter's afternoon in such a manner. Besides which, if you truly were honest about such a declaration, I do not think I would have seen you take part in a single parlor game thus far. There have been many of them, and try as I might, I cannot think of a single one you have absented yourself from as yet."

Unfortunately, no quick response came to Edward. He simply stared back at Miss Moir.

"And yet you will not take part in *this* game, because you consider it juvenile." Shaking her head, Miss Moir looked away from him. "A pity."

"It would not have been sporting of me to refuse to join in with my guests." His abrasive tone appeared to have no effect on the lady, for she merely laughed, her tone a little mocking, before she thrust out one hand in a dismissive gesture. "I highly doubt it is the *only* reason you have joined in such games, Your Grace."

Without another word, she turned on her heel and began to walk away, leaving her last remark hanging in the air between them. Despite the fact he wished very much to make a sharp response, a response that would give him the triumph of having the last word, nothing came to his lips. His attempts to remove his frustration seemed to have failed entirely, for it now redoubled itself. Why ever had his mother thought to invite Miss Moir? Was it because she had seen him speaking pleasantly to her during summer Season? That had only been on one or two occasions, but it did not mean Edward liked the young lady particularly well. His frown grew as he recalled how she had carefully pushed him away when he had made a quiet suggestion they dance together. She had directed him instead towards her friend and had smiled as she had done it. It was strange how that memory still came to him, and how much he was still irritated by it. Why his thoughts should linger on Miss Moir, as they did at this moment, he could give no explanation for – but all the same, he began to question why, during the summer Season, she had seemed so disinclined towards dancing with him.

Muttering to himself, Edward dragged his eyes away from her and began to make his way back into the house. The few small bits of snow on his skin began to melt, sending icy drops down the back of his neck and causing him to grimace. Miss Moir's foolish frivolity meant he would now have to change his clothes.

Unless I stayed out of doors.

Edward stopped, closed his eyes tightly and set his jaw. Where was this sudden desire to linger out of doors coming from? It was not only that, but there was also an eagerness now to take part in the snowball fight – a pastime he had called foolish only a few moments ago! It took such a great hold of him, it was almost impossible to shake off. Edward hesitated, his hand lingering on the rail of the staircase as he stared straight ahead, attempting to push himself away from such idiocy. Why he should want to be out of doors and in the company of Miss Moir he did not know, for had he not only just told himself how much she irritated him? Why then did he have such a strange desire to be close to her?

Taking a deep breath, Edward forced his steps upwards. This had been a most unsettling afternoon – first with a conversation from his mother and now with Miss Moir. The sooner he could be free from it all, the better. He would simply forget Miss Moir as best he could and would make no attempt to further his connection with Miss Williams, so his mother would not attempt to push him all the closer to her. He had made it quite plain to his mother he had no intention of matrimony at the present time. She did not much like it, of course, but he was his own man and he would choose his own path – and, indeed, his own bride – and his mother would simply have to accept his choice, whether she liked the lady or not.

CHAPTER TWO

The ballroom was loud and crowded, but the sound did not bother Augusta at all. Instead, it made her smile. It was a reminder of the summer day during the Season when she had been able to laugh and dance and smile with many of her friends and acquaintances. It was so different now. Summer seemed like a whole lifetime ago, especially now, when the dark nights began to grow a little too solemn, when the air itself seemed to be weighed with a heaviness which only came during the winter season. Augusta did not much care for nights bundled with many blankets for the cold air that nipped at her ears and her toes. She did not much enjoy spending many hours in the same company, for especially now her sister was wed, Augusta was all alone, with only her mother and father for company. The winter season was not inclined to bring much joy and yet now, despite the fact she had no particular interest in the Duke himself, Augusta was glad to be present here at least. There was music, there was dancing, there was laughter and there was happiness – and all this in the midst of a dark winter. How joyous it was to stand here at the very beginnings of what was sure to be an excellent evening.

"I cannot decide which gentleman it is you are studying at present."

With a small start of surprise, Augusta turned to see an acquaintance, Miss Williams, smiling at her.

"I am not looking at any gentleman, I assure you." She gave a wry laugh, which Miss Williams did not appear to believe, given the slight twist to her lips. "In fact, I was just thinking about how pleasant an evening this is sure to be."

"It is going to be an excellent evening, especially with all these very fine gentleman present." Miss Williams smiled. "The Duke of Meyrick is the epitome of a fine gentleman, is he not?" Tilting her head, she sighed happily and, in doing so, reminded Augusta very much of her friend, Miss Keen. "He is so very handsome."

"I have heard many people say so and thus, I assume, it must be true." The dry remark flung itself forward before Augusta could prevent it, and the gasp that followed from Miss Williams sent heat searing into Augusta's face. She ought not to have been so forward, so thoughtless. Miss Williams could easily repeat what she had said to someone else, perhaps even to the Duke.

"That is not to say I do not think him handsome also," she continued quickly as Miss Williams's open mouth closed again. "I only mean to remark upon how almost everyone I speak to mentions how handsome the Duke of Meyrick is."

"But of course they should!" Miss Williams' surprise had not quite left her, her eyes flashing a little. "And I must say *I* think him exceptionally so, and I am certain you do also, even if you will not admit it aloud." The flash of her eyes faded. "But then again, I believe it is a requirement for every Duke to be handsome."

This final sentence was said with a light lilt to Miss Williams' voice, and a smile which brought immediate relief to Augusta. "Certainly if a Duke *can* be handsome, then he certainly must try to be," she agreed softly. "Do you know the gentleman well?"

"No, I do not." Miss Williams' sigh spoke of a wistfulness. "I had hoped our acquaintance would approve improve during the house party, but there are so many guests, and he is so very busy." With another sigh, she shook her head. "And I have never once had to offer him a forfeit as yet. I have tried, however, but my machinations have come to naught. Perhaps there shall be another game tomorrow and I can attempt to do so again!"

Augusta remained silent, thinking she would never deliberately attempt to lose a parlor game simply so she would have to face a forfeit, though she was all too aware a good deal of cheating had taken place thus far! The young ladies were attempting to garner attentions by deliberately losing and gentlemen were swapping trinkets in the hope of stealing a kiss from their favorite lady. The thought of offering the Duke a forfeit made Augusta's skin prickle, believing every other young lady would find the idea utterly delightful.

"From your presence and expression, might I assume you do not particularly enjoy the parlor games?" Miss Williams smiled at her. "You did seem to be enjoying playing out in the snow, however."

"I certainly did enjoy it, yes." Having no qualms about sharing such a thing, Augusta smiled back at Miss Williams. "It is a game where one can only be fair. There is no cheating or deviation and there are no forfeits required. All in all, I found it a good deal more favorable than other games."

"We are very different in that regard. I confess I am much more inclined towards seeking out forfeits." Her eyes practically glowed. "It brings with it such wonderful moments."

Augusta only nodded, finding she could not agree. It is not expected for her to concur, however, and they passed the next few minutes in near silence, simply watching all that took place.

It was Miss Williams who broke the quiet first.

"For all that you may not be inclined towards the Duke of Meyrick, he certainly appears to be inclined towards you."

The remark was so astonishing, Augusta gave a start, turning wide eyes towards Miss Williams. "I do not understand what you mean."

Miss Williams laughed, as though she believed Augusta was being deliberately obtuse. "I am certain you do," she remarked, sending a sliding glance to her left. "Surely it is obvious he is watching you at present."

Blinking in astonishment, Augusta's heart began to hammer furiously as she dared a glance across the room. For whatever reason, her gaze snagged immediately on the Duke of Meyrick, making it clear that Miss Williams was quite correct in her statement. The moment their gazes met, the Duke immediately turned his away, leaving her all the more embarrassed and with it, a little confused. Why should he be looking at her? Their last conversation had not gone particularly well. Firstly, she had embarrassed herself by hitting him with the snowball, and secondly, she had managed to argue with him instead of merely apologizing.

"I think you quite mistaken, Miss Williams." Forcing a

smile, she gestured vaguely in the Duke of Meyrick's direction. "There is no certainty as to who exactly the Duke is looking at. It may be he was gazing at you."

This flattery seemed to please Miss Williams, for her smile lifted all the more and a gentle flush ran across her cheeks. "Mayhap you are right, Miss Moir!" She looked across the room at him again whilst Augusta fixed her gaze steadily upon her acquaintance. "Perhaps I am to be the lucky one. Perhaps he will show me some attentions this evening."

"I do hope he will."

As though the Duke of Meyrick had heard them speaking, once the current dance ended, he immediately came towards them both. His gaze danced from one to the other, as though he could not decide as to who he ought to rest his eyes upon.

"Good evening, Miss Moir, Miss Williams." His smile was brief. "I do hope you are both enjoying the ball this evening?"

The gentleman did not have to wait for the reply to come, for Miss Williams was just as eager as Miss Keen had been during the summer season.

"Oh yes, Your Grace. The ball is delightful. Out of all I have attended, it is the most wonderful." She laughed and flapped one hand in his direction. "I am sure *all* of the balls you host are just as magnificent, however, and therefore, it is such an honor to be invited not only to this evening, but to your entire house party. You cannot know how much it has pleased me and how grateful I am to you for your invitation."

Augusta let out a slow breath, wondering when it might be that Miss Williams would draw breath, and watching as the Duke's smile also slowly began to die away.

"But of course."

Interrupting just as soon as he could, the Duke then turned his attention obviously towards Augusta. "And are you enjoying it also, Miss Moir?"

"I am." She said nothing more, looking back steadily into the Duke's face and aware of how his eyebrows drew low over his eyes. Was he expecting her to make further conversation? To speak as eagerly as Miss Williams had done? If he was, she considered, he would be sorely disappointed.

"Then might I ask if you would both be willing to offer me your dance cards?"

It came as no surprise to Augusta that Miss Williams was instantly ready with such a thing, slipping it from her wrist and handing it to the Duke within only a moment. Augusta herself watched as he glanced over it, having no intention of giving him her dance card unless he asked for it specifically. Perhaps stepping out with Miss Williams would be quite enough.

The Duke lifted his head. "And you also, Miss Moir?"

Augusta held back her sigh with an effort. She could not escape from him this time. She could not suggest he step out with Miss Williams only, which meant there was naught for her to do but to accept. Rather frustrated, she slipped it from her wrist and handed it to him, catching the way his lips curved, as if he were glad he had managed to force her into giving him her dance card. The Duke's eyes dropped to the card as he took it, studying it for a short while. He smiled as he dotted his name down before offering it back to her, his smile still lingering.

"What say you to the waltz, Miss Moir?"

Augusta did not believe him at first, looking down at her dance card to confirm whether he was speaking the truth.

To her utter astonishment, she saw his name was, in fact, in the space for her waltz, meaning she would be stepping out with the Duke of Meyrick for the most important dance of the evening. Why had he decided to take her waltz, knowing all of his guests, his mother and, of course, her own mother also, would notice his particular choice? It would bring attention to them both – attention she did not want.

"Are you quite certain, Your Grace?"

"More than that, Miss Moir, I am determined." The Duke smiled, but there was still a sharpness in his gaze. "This should make up for the summer Season when I did not manage to step out with you even once."

Still struggling to understand his intentions, Augusta merely shrugged and turned her face away. "Very well, Your Grace. If it is your wish, then of course." She threw him a quick glance alongside a cool smile, silently wondering if there was something more to this waltz, something more than he intended for it. Regardless, however, Augusta could not escape for it. She was to dance the waltz with the Duke of Meyrick.

"You do not make much conversation, Miss Moir."

Augusta lifted her chin and looked directly into the Duke's eyes. They had been waltzing for only a minute at the very most, but already he was to converse. His arm was tight around her waist, his grip strong. "I am concentrating on my steps, Your Grace, so I do not make any mistakes. I should be highly embarrassed if I were to put a foot in the wrong place!"

"I see. I am glad you have stepped out with me, Miss Moir."

"I did not think I had much of a choice." She tore her eyes away from him for a moment, a curl of frustration growing within her belly. "It is not often young ladies are able to refuse a gentleman, Your Grace, particularly if the gentleman who requires a dance is a Duke."

The gentleman did not appear to be at all upset by her remark, for he grinned as a bark of laughter broke from him. "I suppose your statement is true, though you *did* refuse me during the summer Season. You were unable to use the same ploy this evening, however!" He continued to dance and, at the very next moment, swung her sharply to the left.

Augusta caught her breath, her hand holding fast to his, unable to understand what the Duke was doing. Her breath returned to her, only to be stolen away again as the Duke came to a stand them both directly underneath a kissing bough.

"Miss Moir." The Duke loosened his arm from about her waist, stepping a little away from the rest of the dancers. "It seems as though we are underneath a kissing bough. Whatever shall we do?"

Immediately Augusta's face flamed, her fingers curling into her palms. Was this his intention? Had he thought to embarrass her by stopping underneath a kissing bough, knowing almost every eye would be upon them? Or was he seeking to garner a reaction from her, in the hope that she might then behave as every other young lady did towards him? With a sniff, she looked away. "I believe we *are* able to ignore it, Your Grace."

"Good gracious, Miss Moir. Are you unwilling to offer your kiss to someone such as I?"

Augusta's jaw tightened. The Duke was clearly seeking either to discomfit her or, by his teasing charms, to make her as pliable as other young ladies of his acquaintance. She would do neither, however. Her eyebrow arched despite the fact her face continued to burn. "Certainly I am not, Your Grace. I should not dare to do such a thing." Tipping her chin up, she stood there patiently, waiting – and the Duke's expression began to shift. The confidence in her tone had his smile beginning to crumble, the light disappearing from his eyes. The waltz continued around them, music sweeping the other couples by them, and still the Duke did not move.

Augusta smiled inwardly. She was not about to flush and look away in a great state of awkwardness, as perhaps he had imagined. She was not about to clasp her hands to her heart, so overcome with a great ravage of emotion at the thought of kissing him, she could no longer even breathe. Neither reaction would be hers. She was determined. She was steady, and had enough inner strength to remain composed, no matter what took place.

At the very next moment, the Duke dropped his head and his lips were pressed to hers. It was only for the briefest of moments, a feather touch, and yet her response to it was so utterly extraordinary, Augusta could not seem to recover. Not a single thought was constructed, her breath refusing to pull from her lungs as her eyes opened to gaze up at the gentleman who had fired such a response in her. The Duke was blinking rapidly, his own face suddenly expressionless, perhaps suggesting that, though he had expected to feel some great triumph, he now was dealing with something quite the opposite. The more he stared at her, the more Augusta could not seem to move from her position, her whole self freezing into position, from her toes to the very top of her head.

"You have missed the end of the waltz, Your Grace!" Lord Burton's voice broke them both apart as a shiver ran over Augusta's skin. Stepping back, she bobbed a quick curtsy and then hurried away, before the Duke had opportunity to say another word to her. She did not look to her left, nor to her right, did not look for her mother, nor for her friend, Lady Rebecca, nor for Miss Williams. Instead, she made her way directly to the door, walking out of the ballroom, scurrying along the hallway until she found an empty room. Stepping inside, she slammed the door behind her and sagged against it. One arm wrapped around her waist, her eyes closing, her chin dropping to her chest as she dragged in breath after breath, trying to calm the frantic beating of her heart. Everything which had flitted through her in that one single moment was more extraordinary, more overwhelming than she had ever experienced in her life before and all because of the Duke of Meyrick's kiss – a gentleman in whom she had very little interest in, very little consideration for. Why, then, had she felt herself so overcome? Why had her desire been to lean into his arms? It was far too difficult for her to understand, and thus Augusta kept her eyes closed, concentrating only on her steady breathing as her feelings slowly began to ebb away.

Whatever she had thought this evening would bring, she had never even imagined such a moment with the Duke. The desire to return to the ball and to dance with other gentleman was quite gone from her, and thus Augusta made up her mind to quit the ball entirely. Once she was recovered enough, she would return to her bedchamber and perhaps take to her bed, choosing to read instead of dancing through the evening and into the early hours of the following morning. She did not want to see the Duke again, not this evening, not until she was able to compose herself. His kiss had unsettled her so deeply, Augusta feared it would take her some time to recover.

CHAPTER THREE

"And what devious game has your mother concocted for us this evening?"

Edward slid his gaze towards Lord Ossington. "I believe we are to play Hot Cockles."

At this, Lord Ossington's eyes flared with a sudden expectant light as a broad grin settled over his features. "An excellent game!" he chuckled as the other gentleman laughed. They had all enjoyed an excellent dinner, and now sat together at the table with their port in hand, waiting for the Duke to decide when they might go to join the ladies in the drawing room. Edward himself was in no particular rush. After the ball last evening, he had found himself rather tired, although the strange moment with Miss Moir was still haunting him whenever he allowed his thoughts to turn to it.

"I do think it a favorite parlor game." Lord Kensington grinned broadly, lifting his port glass to his lips. "Although I have never understood why one must sit in the lap of another. One could easily be tapped with a stick from their own seat."

"Yes, I suppose that is quite true, but I, for one, am not about to complain!" said another gentleman, as the entire group then dissolved into laughter. Edward found himself grinning, fully aware his desire was to turn his thoughts to what it would be like to have Miss Moir sitting in his lap, but by sheer strength of will, he refused to let them move in that direction. Taking a deep breath, he threw back the rest of the port and then reached to add a little more to his glass. He was not eager to make his way to the drawing room to join with the ladies, not as yet. It would mean he would once more be in company with Miss Moir and, given how much he was fighting to keep her from his mind, he wished to hold it from himself for a little longer.

Their shared moment last evening still tore through him whenever he had even the briefest moment to consider it. First, he had been pleased to take her waltz, thinking he would lead her to the kissing bough during their time together. His expectation had been either she would be highly embarrassed at his actions, especially when she had shown no inclination to further their acquaintance, or that the desire to be kissed by a Duke would finally reveal itself *if*, as he had wondered, such a desire was hidden deep within her. Neither of his expected responses had taken place, however. When he had stopped at the kissing bough, Edward had waited for Miss Moir to drop her eyes, her face to flush and her head to drop, but instead, she had lifted her chin and looked directly at his face without even a flicker of emotion in her expression. There had not been even an ounce of embarrassment nor of overwhelming desire. She had appeared to be quite calm and thus, with his own embarrassment growing, he had not had any other choice but to drop his head and touch his lips to hers - albeit very briefly. And yet, when he had so, the extraordinary whirlwind of emotions which had tangled through him had left him both dumbfounded and frozen in position. Whenever he so much as glanced at the lady today – as he had done many times over the last few hours – Edward had found himself aware of the very same sensations flooding him... and had become deeply frustrated with it.

"I do look forward to sitting on Miss Williams' lap." A coarse laugh ripped from the gentleman to Edward's left, but strangely, no other person joined in. The sound gradually faded to nothing, making Edward lift his head. Glancing around, he caught one or two murmurs, saw the frowns rather than the smiles, and immediately realized the gentleman's concerns. No doubt they had heard something from his mother as regarded Miss Williams – even if it had been only a whisper, it would have been enough to take hold. Rolling his eyes, he looked from one gentleman to the next, then laughed and lifted up his glass of port.

"My dear Lord Montrose, I wish you the very best of luck for this evening. May you either get to sit on Miss Williams' lap, or may she be directed to sit on yours." Noticing the glances between the gentlemen, as well as one or two uncertain smiles, Edward took a sip of his port, then set the glass back on the table. "I can assure you all I have no specific interest at all in Miss Williams. I am also well aware my mother might have made some suggestion as regards the lady, but I am here to tell you all now: I have no desire to court any young lady – and that includes Miss Williams herself. I intend to play each and every parlor game without any desire to steal attentions from anyone in particular, which leaves you quite free to pursue Miss Williams if you so wish, Lord Montrose."

The murmur of relief which ran around the table made Edward shake his head, picking up his port and swirling it around the glass. He did not want anyone to think he had any intention of allowing Lady Meyrick to guide his interests. He would take part in every parlor game, simply to confirm – both to himself and his guests - that he would show no particular favor to *any* young lady. And, as he had done so now, he would encourage Lord Montague and his attention to Miss Williams.

But what of Miss Moir?

The thought came quickly, making Edward wince. Why ever was he thinking about Miss Moir? There was no reason for him to have any consideration of her. Yes, he had some strange, unsettling feelings during their brief kiss last evening, but he could easily dismiss them, could he not? It was deeply frustrating how often she seemed to creep back into the edge of his thoughts.

"Come then." Pushing himself up from his chair, he gestured to the door. "I do not think it would be fair to keep Lord Montrose from Miss Williams. Let us go and play this ridiculously foolish game my mother has devised for us, in the hope we may have many a pretty young lady sat upon our laps."

At this, the gentlemen cheered almost as one, immediately leaping from their chairs before hurrying to the door. Edward stepped back, one hand still out towards the door, encouraging them to go out ahead of him. Letting out a slow breath, he followed after the last into the hallway, only for Lord Hammersmith to step close to him.

"You are quite certain there is nothing between yourself and Miss Williams, then?"

Edward chuckled, giving his friend a wry smile. "I assure you, there is not. My mother is eager for Miss Williams to be of interest to me, whereas I am determined she should not be."

"Is there any reason why Lady Meyrick is pushing you to her?"

Edward threw up his hands, meandering after the rest of the gentleman. "She and Miss Williams' mother, Lady Jefferson, have long been friends, so it may simply be an idea which has come to them both. Regardless, it is not something I am willing to accept at present."

"I see. It must be very trying indeed to have so many young ladies eager for your company." This remark was given with a wry tone to Lord Hammersmith's voice.

"Alas, not *all* young ladies."

Where such a remark had come from, Edward could not say, but instantly his thoughts flung back in the direction of Miss Moir. With a hoarse laugh, he threw aside the statement, seeing his friend's curious glance. To his relief, however, they soon reached the drawing room and he was able to step inside without continuing on the conversation. The room was already filled with laughter. Many of the gentlemen had seated themselves beside a lady whom they favored, whilst Edward himself stood with his hands behind his back, refusing to look at any one lady over another. His chin lifted, and he turned his gaze from one person to the next, rather than looking at anyone for too long. Try as he might, however, he could not help but notice where Miss Moir sat. His attention was stolen by her, his breathing quickening – but his mother rising to her feet brought a calmness to him again.

"For those who wish to, we are to play a game."

Edward could not help but smile at the way Lord Montrose's face lit up. He knew exactly what was coming.

"We will play 'Hot Cockles'," Lady Meyrick continued, smiling. "I am sure everyone knows how to play, so for those who wish to do so, shall we gather our chairs in a circle? My son will fetch the blindfold and the bamboo cane."

Seeing his mother glance at him, Edward nodded, recalling that the blindfold had been placed in a drawer in the library with the cane beside it. Hurrying quickly to fetch it, he left his mother to sort out the game.

By the time he returned, the guests were all seated in a circle with one chair left vacant for him. He took it quickly, barely glancing at the person on either side of him, handing the blindfold and the stick to his mother.

"Thank you." She waved her arms wide. "Now, we shall select someone to be blindfolded, and thereafter the gentlemen or the lady in question will be seated on someone else's lap. Once they are seated, I will choose two or three of you to stand near to the blindfolded person and you must greet them in your own voice. Once introduced, one of you tap the blindfolded person with our cane, and they shall have to guess as to which of you has done it. We are all aware by now, surely, that there will be consequences for those who do not manage to guess correctly?!"

A murmur of laughter echoed around the room, and Edward found himself grinning. It was the most ridiculous game, of course, but no-one seemed to mind – least of all himself! After all, he would get to sit on a pretty young lady's lap, or a young lady would seat themselves on his lap instead. There might be consequences, but the consequences would be nothing more than a chosen dance or a momentary kiss.

What if I was to ask for another kiss from Miss Moir?

Edward found himself on his feet. "It would be sporting if I was the first to play, would it not?"

His mother's eyebrows rose in obvious surprise, only for Edward to shrug his shoulders. His mother returned his gesture with a beaming smile and stretched out one hand towards him.

"You see? The Duke has stepped forward to be the very first participant. Now the question is: who shall I ask to stand before him?" This was said twinkling smile, and Edward accepted the blindfold from his mother, quickly wrapping it over his eyes. A gentle but firm hand grasped his arm and he allowed his mother to lead him around for circle. A little disorientated, he had very little idea as to whose lap he was guided to. Edward sat gingerly, attempting not to put his entire weight onto the young lady as he sat on her lap. There came a squeal from behind him, followed by a good deal of laughter as Edward laughed along with them, waiting for the next part of the game to begin.

"Now, might you step forward, good Sir? And you also, young lady, and you also." Still directing the game, Lady Meyrick chose the next three participants. "I shall hand one of you this cane... here you are."

"You must also greet me, recall."

"But do not give your names," his mother added quickly. "You may greet him, certainly, but that is all."

Waiting patiently, Edward tilted his head a little, as if it might help him to hear them a little better.

"Good evening, Your Grace."

"A very good evening it is, Your Grace."

"It is a very pleasant evening, is it not, Your Grace?"

Edward frowned. Two ladies and one gentleman – but he could not recognize the young ladies very well. The gentleman, he was sure, was Lord Montrose.

"Very well. Greetings have been completed and now you must brace yourself, Your Grace."

A grin replaced his frown. "I am prepared."

There was a breath of silence, and then something hard hit hard against the back of his hand. It was not a gentle tap as he had expected, but rather so sharp, he let out a yelp of surprise and got to his feet. The room immediately burst into laughter, perhaps thinking he was merely play acting, whilst Edward resisted the urge to rub at the back of his hand with the other. He did not want anyone to think him a weakling, but that strike had been a good deal more painful than he had been prepared for.

"The tap has been given, and now you must guess which of the three before you struck your hand!"

Scowling, Edward licked his lips, attempting to push away the throb of pain and concentrate on the task before him. The gentleman was none other than Lord Montrose, he was sure of it, but as for the young ladies, he had very little idea as to who they were.

"Come, you must give us your guess!" His mother's laughter did nothing to help Edward, and he was tempted just to say any name that came to him, only for an idea to strike at him so hard, he caught his breath. Of course! There was only one young lady who would have the audacity to strike him so. One young lady who would dare to do such a thing – and that young lady *had* to be Miss Moir.

"I have my guess." His confidence must have shone through his voice, for the room suddenly went very quiet, to the point it took a few silent seconds before his mother responded.

"Very well. Who had the cane?"

Something rippled around the room – was it laughter? Or anticipation as to who he was going to name? Taking a breath, Edward grinned.

"I believe the person who struck me was Miss Moir."

Immediately, the room was filled with the buzzing of conversation and, again, some more laughter.

"Then why do you not take off your blindfold and see?"

Still filled with confidence, Edward pulled off the blindfold, quite certain he would see none other than Miss Moir with the cane in her hand. The two young ladies and Lord Montrose stood in front of him, their hands behind their backs. Miss Moir was looking at him steadily. There was no smile on her lips, but nor was there a frown either, keeping her face devoid of anything right might give away her current feelings.

"So, as you see, we have Lord Montrose, we have Miss Moir and we have Lady Amelia." Lady Meyrick gestured to one after the other. "Lord Montrose, might you show the Duke your hands?"

With great deliberation, Lord Montrose took first one and then the other hand from behind his back, revealing them to be empty. Those watching began to laugh as Edward grinned, believing he was corrected and delighted that now, he would win the round and therefore have triumph over Miss Moir.

"Miss Moir." In a slightly singsong voice, Lady Meyrick gestured for the young lady to hold out her hands. Excitement billowed as Edward held his breath, ready to exclaim aloud with delight over his success, only for Miss Moir to laugh and then hold out empty hands. The mirth which came from her seemed to set alight everyone else in the room all over again, which grew all the more in resonance as Lady Amelia waved the stick around gently in front of him.

"No..."

Edward breathed the word aloud, his eyes going from Lady Amelia to Miss Moir. "I was sure I..."

"It appears as though you are mistaken, Your Grace."

Miss Moir smiled as Edward shot a sharp look towards his mother. These parlor games were well known for cheating, which meant, mayhap, Miss Moir and Lady Alberta had swapped the cane from one to the other *after* he had guessed her name. His mother, however, merely shook her head, her eyes dancing with obvious delight as the rest of the room roared with merriment at his confusion.

"What else is there to say, my dear son, other than you are mistaken?"

"And you must offer a forfeit to Miss Moir for blaming her for something she did not do," Lord Montrose added, a broad smile on his face. "Either that or face a consequence!"

"There is always the coal fire!" another gentleman shouted as Edward scowled, hating the idea of having coal dust smudged across his face. Sighing inwardly, he looked back to Miss Moir.

"It seems as though I am mistaken." With a slight lift of his eyebrow, he held Miss Moir's gaze steadily, but the lady did not so much as flinch. Instead, the edge of her mouth began to creep up as he took out a clean handkerchief from his pocket and offered it to her. She accepted it with a nod but nothing more, turning back so she might go and sit in her own seat. Edward watched her steadily, quite certain some sort of trickery had taken place, but aware he could never be sure.

Defeated, his shoulders slumped as the lady on whose lap he had sat now rose from her chair, now chosen to be the one blindfolded.

"I have not injured you in any way, I hope?" Turning his head, Edward's stomach lurched upon seeing the smiling face of Miss Williams. No doubt his mother had done such a thing purposefully but he could not permit himself to appear frustrated over that, not here in company.

"Not at all, Your Grace." She held out one hand. "Might I have the blindfold?"

"No, no, Miss Williams, allow the Duke to tie for you. He will oblige you, of course."

Fighting to keep the scowl from his face, Edward did as he was asked; Miss Williams standing quietly before him as he did so.

"Thank you, Your Grace."

"You are most welcome. May you fare better than I in this game."

"I think I shall."

Someone snorted with laughter and instantly, Miss Williams flung one hand to her mouth, her face a gentle pink, and Edward immediately knew he had been duped. With a forced smile, he made his way back across the room to sit down in his chair, his eyes going to Miss Moir. She was sitting quietly, her hands in her lap, but his handkerchief twined between her fingers. When she caught his eye, only a flickering smile was in answer to his exasperated look, leaving Edward in a pit of slow growing frustration.

CHAPTER FOUR

"I saw what you did to the Duke."

Augusta hid her smile, flaring her eyes wide. "I do not know what you mean, Miss Williams."

"I am certain you do," the lady laughed, her arm through Augusta's as they continued to walk across the grass, following after the Duke, his mother and the rest of the guests on their afternoon stroll. "You did hit the Duke rather hard, although at least Lady Amelia seemed very pleased indeed to take the stick from you."

Augusta laughed, aware her guilt had been obvious to almost everyone in the room. "I am afraid I could not help myself." Her eyes went to the Duke himself as he walked ahead of them, his feet taking long strides. "It was rather delightful to play such a trick on him."

Miss Williams laughed with her, the tinkling sound catching the Duke's attention, for he glanced over his shoulder towards them both, only to twist his head away again.

"I believe he is aware something secretive took place, but I do not think that anyone will tell him outright."

"No, I do not think they will, given so many of them have done the very same thing."

Augusta allowed herself a broad smile. "I have the Duke's handkerchief as forfeit also, of course. It does seem a little unfair to have cheated him out of it but it could not be helped! I did not want to have *my* face smudged with coal dust!"

"Quite right." Miss Williams giggled. "And what is it you shall ask of him?" Her voice dropped low as she pulled herself a little closer to Augusta in a most surreptitious manner.

Speaking honestly, Augusta shrugged one shoulder. "I do not know as yet. I must think on it for a little while longer."

For a moment, the thought of asking the Duke for another kiss came to her, but she quickly plucked it from herself and threw it away. "I think I shall keep a hold of his handkerchief for a short while," she continued. "I will confess to liking the fact I have something over the Duke of Meyrick, even if it is very wicked of me to say so."

Miss Williams squeezed her arm. "I quite understand your feelings."

Augusta's smile faded, aware of the guilt that stole some of her merriment. She had not intended to strike the Duke so hard but seeing him sitting there with that broad smile on his face had irritated her, and thus she had tapped his hand with a little too much force, as though he were an unruly child requiring chastisement. The other guests had found this marvelously entertaining, and she had not felt any guilt whatsoever at cheating. Even now, a small bubble of laughter pushed itself up within her, recalling the confusion in his face when he had spoken her name so proudly, only to be told she did not have the cane.

"The Duke is looking at you again, Miss Moir."

Augusta blinked, quickly returning to the conversation with Miss Williams. "Is he?" She waved her free hand dismissively. "No doubt he is wondering – as you are – what I shall ask from him in exchange for his handkerchief."

"Or mayhap there may also be a little more interest in you than you are willing to see."

Aware of the slight flush now growing in her cheeks, Augusta quickly shook her head. "I do not think you are correct, Miss Williams." Again, she glanced at the Duke, only to see him looking over his shoulder at her again. When their eyes met, she quickly pulled hers away. "I am not so foolish as to think anything of his attention, given what has only just passed last evening."

"You do not wish for the Duke's interest?"

Augusta let out a slow breath, wondering whether or not she ought to be truthful with the lady. "I am well aware every young lady is eager for the Duke of Meyrick to pay heed to them, but I confess I am not one so inclined. I care very little as to whether or not the Duke pays any attention to me whatsoever. I am simply glad to be here and am enjoying the house party a great deal."

"That is very honest of you, Miss Moir," Miss Williams remarked, still a smile playing about her mouth. "I think, however, the Duke may garner the attention of *any* young lady, regardless of whether she wishes to give it. You may find yourself soon caught by him, even if you are determined not to allow him to snag your interest." With those parting words and a wave to Miss Harding, Miss Williams stepped away from Augusta, leaving her to walk alone for a short time while she went to walk with Miss Harding instead. Augusta did not hurry after her nor seek to find someone else to walk with, but rather allowed those final words to penetrate her mind. There was something deeply unsettling about those words, for they reminded her that there was, in fact, a certain degree of interest in the Duke – but her interest only came from her desire to show him her complete disinterest.... was it not? Her lips tugged to one side as she considered, her teeth catching her lip.

"Why are you walking alone, Augusta?" Her mother's sharp tone caught Augusta unawares, and she jumped slightly, seeing her mother now scurrying towards her. "It does not look as though you are having any enjoyment whatsoever."

Augusta offered her mother a small smile. "I assure you, I am."

"Then why are you walking without company?" her mother demanded, as though to do so was a dreadful thing indeed.

"I was merely contemplating-"

"Might I suggest you contemplate when you are alone in your bedchamber," her mother interrupted, a little brusquely. "Do hurry up. I have heard it said that today, the Duke is eager to speak with you and now, here you are, as far away from him as can be!"

Augusta rolled her eyes at this, believing her mother was only saying such a thing in order to get her to hurry her steps. Lady Sutton grasped Augusta's arm tightly, her voice a low hiss.

"I am being quite serious. He was overheard speaking about you with Lord Montrose. Have you spoken to him today?"

Augusta sighed aloud, making her mother's lips flatten. "I am certain, as I have said only a few moments ago, he speaks of me due to the fact I hold his handkerchief and will require something from him by way of forfeit. He will wonder what it is I will ask. I do not think we need to make anything of it."

"Well, *you* may not think so, but I certainly do," came her mother's quick response. "One should never pass up the opportunity to be spoken of by a Duke nor to be in his company. The former means he is thinking of you."

Thinking it useless to argue, Augusta gave her mother a smile and then hid it away quickly. Yet again, her mother was attempting to push her in one direction she was determined to turn from – even if her foolish heart seemed eager to do otherwise.

""I HAVE NOTHING FOR YOU."

Augusta stopped suddenly, one hand pressing against her heart as the Duke's harsh tones lifted through the air towards her. She ought not to be eavesdropping, of course, but she had been making her way from the staircase to the drawing room when the Duke's loud voice had suddenly become very clear indeed.

"But it is St Thomas' Day!" The broken voice of another reached Augusta's ears and she frowned, deciding to hurry past the Duke's study, the small parlor and towards the Duke himself rather than turning to the direction of the drawing room. Her eyes settled on him, her heart pounding furiously as he threw out one hand in the direction of the three women who stood in the thoroughfare, clearly urging them back towards the door.

"I am aware – and yet, I believe, have given to you already. You ought not to come asking for more."

The sharp exclamation which pulled from Augusta's lips was silenced only by her hand flying to her mouth. St Thomas'

Day was when those who were blessed with wealth, gave to those who were not, aiding them by monetary or physical means to sustain themselves through the winter. It was a life Augusta could not even imagine. Why, then, was the Duke of Meyrick being so very harsh? The 21st of December was a day when he ought to have expected the poor in the vicinity of the estate to come calling and to hear him pushing these ladies away now was most distressing indeed. Yes, even if they had come calling once already, was his wealth not so great he could not offer them something more? They were obviously desperate.

"As I have said, I have nothing for you." Again, he made a frantic waving motion with his hand, pushing the older women and the two others back towards the door. "Pray, remove yourselves from my house."

Augusta made her way purposefully towards him, clearing her throat in an obvious manner so the Duke could hear her approach. His gaze did turn towards her, but his expression remained dark, a storm building in his eyes.

"Goodness, I had quite forgot it is St Thomas' Day." She offered a smile to the three women who stood before herself and the Duke, taking in three faces which were pinched with the cold. Their clothes were thin, their shawls patched and the red of their cheeks and blue of their lips spoke of the cold. How could the Duke turn them away with nothing?

"I have given to you already. Do not think you will garner any of my sympathy simply because Miss Moir has arrived. I will not give to the same people twice." His harsh tones grated on Augusta's heart, her breath hitching at the fury in his gaze. Whatever was the matter with him?

Taking a deep breath, she forced herself to behave properly and offered a smile to the three women. It would not do to speak badly to the Duke in front of them, and she certainly could not *think* of berating him in any way. "I see." Her gaze again went to the three women – no doubt they were all widows and even more impoverished than others around them. Why was the Duke being so unsympathetic? She could not imagine how cold they must be at present, and no doubt they had no roaring fire and the very best of food waiting for them, as she and the Duke did. It was an unenviable existence.

One of the women shivered violently, tears in her gaze as she looked back at Augusta as though she were her very last hope – and anger began to break through Augusta's careful poise.

"Your Grace." Turning her attention back to the Duke, she looked up at him in the calm manner she had perfected given her many years of training. It did not do to lose one's temper in company, despite how angry one might be feeling. "It is St Thomas' Day, is it not?"

The Duke drew himself up. Standing tall, his arms crossing over his chest, his cheeks beginning to flush red as his eyes narrowed. "I am well aware of the date, Miss Moir." With a curl of his lip, he sniffed and turned his gaze away. "These three have arrived here already and were offered some coin. I –"

"We gave those to those we know who cannot leave their homes, due to infirmity!" one lady exclaimed, stepping forward, her eyes now sparking with tears also. "I am ashamed to come and ask again, but we have no other choice."

Augusta's heart billowed with sympathy, her eyes turning back to the Duke – only to see the jut of his jaw and the tightness of his frame.

"I believe I have made myself quite clear. Good evening."

Without another word, he turned on his heel and strode along the hallway, leaving Augusta to stand with the three impoverished ladies as a cold, icy wind blew through the bottom of the front door.

Much like his heart.

Forcing a smile, she turned back to the three women, fully aware they were all now looking at her expectantly. She could do very little – but she would do what she could. She had a few coins, certainly, and every one of them would go to these three ladies who needed so much more than she.

"The Duke may not be able to offer you very much, but I do have some coins I can fetch for you." It was all she could do, and the three ladies immediately let out exclamations of gratitude. Begging them to excuse her for a moment, Augusta turned her heel and hurried back towards the staircase, climbing the steps hastily as she scurried to her bedchamber where her coins were kept. As she walked, her anger billowed with such intensity, it seemed as though her whole body burned. How could the Duke, with all of his wealth and standing, be so inconsiderate to the less fortunate? He was meant to do as much as he could to care for the community around him, and instead he had simply ignored those who needed him the most. Yes, they had been once before but they had given their coins to those who could not leave their homes! Surely that ought to be admired and even rewarded? St Thomas' Day was a day for generosity to be shown in an even greater amount than usual, to those who required it. Instead, the Duke had literally turned his back on them.

Any gentle feelings she had for the Duke quickly burned away to ash. He was harsh and cruel in a way she had not known and had not expected. How could he do such a thing? How could he be so bitter? She had thought he would have, at the very least, a sense of duty, if not generosity of heart. Now it appeared she had entirely misjudged him.

Tipping out her coin purse, she grasped all she had and hurried back, eager to hand the coins to the ladies before the Duke had a chance to return, for fear he would throw them out before she could do so. As she hastened, Augusta passed the Duke's study on her way to the door, only to see the door a little ajar. Thinking she would give the Duke a piece of her mind, she pushed it open, only to find it vacant. Stamping one foot on the floor in irritation, she made to turn back to the door, only for her gaze to catch on something. Moving slowly, she looked over the small corner table, seeing the many ornaments upon it and, at the very back, a small china figurine of a lithe young woman, with a single diamond at her heart.

Her hand reached for it. She ought not take it, hearing her conscience was already plaguing her, but her anger at the Duke grew so furiously that before she knew it, she had picked up the small figure and was making to quit the room.

The three women were still waiting for her.

"Here." She pressed some coins into each lady's hand, and thereafter, handed the small ornament to the first. "I am certain this will be worth something. I do hope it will see you and those you care for, through the winter."

The first lady looked at it, then lifted her gaze slowly back towards Augusta. "Are you sure, Miss? It does look so very expensive." Holding back out the figurine towards Augusta, her red rimmed eyes searched her face, giving Augusta opportunity to take it back from her, should she decide to do so.

A slight snag of doubt caught Augusta's heart, and she took a breath. "I am quite sure." She pressed it again into the lady's hands, aware of the glassy tears which had formed in the lady's eyes. "I do hope it will serve you well."

"May God bless you," came the response of the second lady as the first burst into tears, which then began to stream down her face. "You have saved us. You have saved us all."

Augusta smiled and made to say something, only for the low voice of the Duke to come echoing down the hallway towards her. No doubt he was about to go back to his study, but nonetheless, she ushered the three women outside and then hurriedly closed the door. She did not look behind her, but continued on her way, making as though she were going directly towards the drawing room. Guilt immediately began to twist up inside her, sending her hands into spasm as she clenched and unclenched them, fearful now she had done the wrong thing. Her conscience had barked at her not to take what belonged to the Duke, but nonetheless, she had done so. She had given it to the three women, told them to sell it and to pay for what they required with the coins which had come from it, and she certainly could not chase after them now. It was foolishness to even contemplate it.

"Miss Moir."

The Duke's commanding tone echoed down the hall-way, and Augusta started violently. She stopped walking but stayed precisely where she was, somehow finding it incredibly difficult to glance over her shoulder towards him. The little ornament had been tucked away in the corner of his study and the Duke could not have noticed its absence already.

"Miss Moir, I am well aware you think me harsh, but I have already given coins to those three women. I do not think I – "

"I think you very hard indeed, Your Grace."

The Duke walked straight past her and then swung directly back to face her, his eyes a little narrowed. "I have good reason for doing as I did."

"And what could such reasons be?" Augusta shot back, her fury returning, as though he had set light to already smoldering coals. "It is St Thomas' Day. It is expected of you to be generous, and instead you pull yourself away from them as though they are grasping for no good reason. I could see the hunger in their eyes, I could see how the cold made them tremble, and yet you did not show the smallest amount of compassion."

"As I have said, I gave to them already."

"And they, in turn, gave those coins to those who cannot leave their homes due to infirmity," she fired back, seeing his lips flatten, his gaze drop. "These are people who are within or near to your estate, who must rely on your kindness and the kindness of others in order to make it through the winter in some vague semblance of comfort – and all you can do has thrust them from your door and tell them you have made your decision? Your decision to give them nothing more, I might add, when you and I have so very much. How can you be so cruel hearted?"

The Duke sniffed, looking away from her as though she were being quite ridiculous. "I have responsibilities yes, but those responsibilities do not mean I am compelled to show more generosity than is required."

At this, Augusta threw back her head and glared at him, her hands in tight fists, her voice shaking. "That is exactly what the Season is about, Your Grace. It is a time to be generous of spirit and of heart. We spent many hours here enjoying one another's company, laughing, joking, eating all kinds of wonderful delicacies and delighting in your great wealth. But these three women come asking for a little more, having shared what you already gave them, and you determine *not* to show even the smallest modicum of generosity to those who need it far more than your present house guests."

In response, the Duke of Meyrick dropped his head, flushing scarlet as he did so. After a few moments, he lifted it again and opened his mouth, but no answer came. He could not seem to speak to her and, try as he might, no words passed from his lips. His eyes simply fixed hers, and as the seconds passed, Augusta's heart slowly began to quieten itself. She had said everything she needed to say, save it, for one thing.

"How low you have fallen in my estimation, Your Grace." Her voice was soft now, her head turning away from him. "You know I do not take much interest in the title of a gentleman. I do not consider him simply for his standing, but rather because of his character and alas, Your Grace, whilst you may have excellent standing and incredible wealth, it appears you are lacking in what is the most important."

The fact she had always been brusque with her thoughts and emotions meant Augusta did not rear back from speaking honestly. Her heart was sore as she turned away from him entirely, pulling her gaze away as she silently turned away and headed to her bedchamber,

CHAPTER FIVE

*E*dward poured himself another whisky and threw it back far too hastily. It had been one full day since those poor widows had come to his house, one full day since he had spoken with such harshness, and one full day since Miss Moir had watched him with wide eyes and a white face, clearly appalled at his behavior.

Grimacing, Edward ran one hand over his face, slouching forward over his desk. Now he had time to reflect, now he had opportunity to look back on his behavior, he could understand completely why Miss Moir had reacted in such a fashion. He was heartily ashamed of his response, fully aware it had come from his own self rather than from anything the widows themselves had done. Frustration had built during the conversation with his mother, the slow churn beginning to build it into anger, and thus, he had left his mother's presence with ire burning in his veins. The three widows had come to ask for a few coins, for gifts from him which could be used to help them through what was certain to be a cold and unrelenting winter. Yes, they had come to his door before, but their explanation had been reasonable and, he considered, more than a little generous on their part. The coin he had given them, they had given to others, to those who could not come on their own two feet. Had he responded with any kindness?

No, he had allowed his feelings to come to the fore and had taken what he felt and thrown it at them – and all in front of Miss Moir.

Groaning aloud, he closed his eyes. He did not want company, he did not want to be in amongst his guests, not when he had so much upon his mind. This was a time when he needed to think through what he had done and what he was to do thereafter.

A knock came to his study door, interrupting his solitude. Edward was about to bark an order that he was not to be disturbed, only for his mother's voice to echo through it.

"Our guests are waiting."

Edward's grimace deepened as his mother pushed the door open, unwilling to wait for his response to allow her to enter. "You will join us, surely."

"I have no wish to be in company at present. I will join you in a short while."

His mother did not appear to hear him, for she immediately came into the room and closed the door behind her. Her eyebrows lifted. "You said very little at dinner," she remarked quietly, although no smile came to her face. "I do hope it is not because of our conversations about Miss Williams that you have retreated into yourself so?"

Closing his eyes, Edward waved one hand at his mother. "Please, Mother, do not," he began, only for Lady Meyrick to interrupt him, tenacious as ever.

"You are cross with me for insisting Miss Williams would be an excellent choice of bride. I understand."

Edward dropped his hand to the table, squinting at his

mother as she came to stand in front of his desk. "It is more than being a little cross," he answered, giving her a somewhat pointed look. He waited until she dropped her gaze, which occurred some long moments later.

"And you have still given me no good reason as to why you will not consider her."

The stab of frustration to his heart had him blowing out a slow breath, aware of how tense this conversation was beginning to make him. "And you have given me no good reason as to why I ought to consider her," he stated firmly. "I have told you, I have *pleaded* with you to leave me in peace as regards my own present unmarried situation, but you seem quite determined to force it upon me whether I would have you do so or not. I cannot understand your reasons behind pushing Miss Williams so fervently towards me. There must be a reason behind it, but as yet you will not tell it to me. Therefore I will state quite clearly now, I consider this matter closed." Dropping his head, he prayed quietly his mother would choose to quit the room rather than linger on.

His prayers were not answered.

Lady Meyrick frowned, her brows throwing themselves together, her expression rather heavy, her lips twisting.

"The housekeeper tells me we received at least two dozen widows at the door up yesterday." Her quiet words added even more heaviness to Edward's spirit, reminded again of just how shameful his actions had been. "You gave to them all, I assume?"

Lifting his head, Edward blinked at her, wondering if somehow his mother knew what he had done and if this was her way of driving a knife a little further into her heart, so his guilt might compel him to consider Miss Williams after all.

"Yes, I gave to all... although not to all who requested it from me." His answer brought to gentle lift to his mother's eyebrows, but she did not pursue it any further. Edward' heart burned with shame over thinking so badly of his mother and he ran one hand over his eyes, his gut twisting. Was he to add further shame to himself? Was his conscience not already screaming at him?

"I shall leave you now." In contradiction to her words, Lady Meyrick came closer to him, reaching out to settle her hand on his for a moment. Her eyes were soft, her expression gentle. "I am sorry I have upset you so." There was legitimacy in her tone and in her quiet expression, resulting in Edward' heart sinking even lower.

"You *have* troubled me, mother, with your insistence, but I trust now we will not speak of it any longer."

She nodded but said nothing, a flicker drawing itself across Edward's forehead in the silence. Lady Meyrick pressed her lips together tightly, opened her mouth, shook her head, and then turned towards the door. "I hope you will join the guests soon. I am just about to begin another parlor game. Should I wait for you?"

Edward shook his head. "Please, begin without me." Recognizing he was not in the right mood for games, not when his mind was so heavy, he offered a brief smile. "I shall join you when I am ready. If anyone asks where I am, tell them I am doing a little business."

His mother did not press him any further, but rather allowed him to speak as he wished. With a nod, she quietly left the room, no words of encouragement pushing from her. Edward immediately closed his eyes, greeting the solitude with a great welcome. His greeting did not last for long, however, for soon his thoughts began to turn to Miss Moir and those three poor widows; his guilt returning to settle in him all over again, like an unwelcome friend who never truly took their leave.

I ought never to have behaved so.

Sighing heavily, Edward pinched the bridge of his nose and closed his eyes. He had only just been beginning to enjoy the house party, but such enjoyment had been pulled from him all over again – but this time, solely by his own actions, rather than the actions of his mother or anyone else. Everything Miss Moir had said to him last evening was legitimate. Christmas time was for generosity of both heart and mind and yet, in his anger and frustration, his generosity had worn out. How could such a thing be when he, the Duke of Meyrick, had more than enough? He could give and give and give many times over without ever being in the least bit concerned, so why had he ever allowed himself to behave in such a dishonorable fashion?

Groaning, Edward rose from his chair. There was nothing for him to do other than join his guests. He could not solve any problems by sitting here alone, not when his weighted thoughts were becoming all the heavier. To do so would achieve nothing but leaving him pained and broken. No, it would be best to join the others, and while he had no intention of taking part in any games, he could still be there, present among them. Perhaps that would give him a little respite from his guilt and, thereafter, make the path forward a little clearer.

EDWARD COULD NOT HELP but watch Miss Moir, even though he told himself silently he ought to be doing everything he could to keep his gaze from her. The hope his guilt would lessen when he was with his guests quickly faded, for every time Miss Moir so much as glanced near to him, the weight of his decision clamped down upon his shoulders all over again.

Miss Moir had shown more kindness and compassion than he had done. There had been more of a willingness to consider what the widows told her, more of a desire to listen and to understand those poor women's circumstances. How sharp her words had been when she had rebuked him for falling short! He did not believe any other young woman of his acquaintance would dare to do such a thing as that, but Miss Moir had not held herself back. Deep within him, something about it made him admire her. It was an admiration he did not want to feel, certainly, a desire he was desperate to push away, but it lingered there all the same.

His head dropped low, his heart growing heavier still as he thought about how she had stood in the hallway and told him everything which he ought to have done. Every single word had been flung at him, had scratched and stabbed at his heart, but it had been true, nonetheless. Yes, he ought to have been a good deal more generous and considerate. He ought to have been able to set aside his anger and frustration and speak kindly to those who had so very little compared to him. It was shameful now to see how he had behaved.

Somehow I must fix this.

Exactly what he would do, Edward was not yet sure. He did not know the names of the three widows, so how was he to find those who had come to his door? Those three widows had not been the first. There had been many who had arrived on St Thomas' Day, and he had given money to all who had asked. Why he had held back from his final three was beyond his comprehension, for their explanation about what they had done with their first gift of coins had been reasonable – and even if it had not, would it have been so difficult to give them a little more? He ought not to have been cruel hearted. The shame of it was heavy on him, tying itself like a noose around his neck so he could not free himself.

"You cannot take your eyes away from her, can you?"

Edward immediately started, looking to his right as his friend smiled knowingly. "I am in the depths of contemplation," Edward responded quickly. "I am not looking at anyone in particular."

Lord Hammersmith chuckled and shook his head. "Very well. We shall pretend you were *not* looking at Miss Moir and have *not* been gazing at her for the last few minutes," he responded with a grin. "Even though I have seen you watch her, we shall pretend otherwise."

Edward snorted and shook his head.

"However, let us also recall that I am your friend and if you wish to tell me something about your feelings as regards the lady, then –"

"I have no feelings." A sharp response was enough to make him appear much too eager, and at his friend's chuckle, Edward only dropped his head and groaned aloud.

"It is just as well no one can hear us speak so openly," Lord Hammersmith remarked, as the game continued around them. "Someone would have heard you groan had they been paying attention and would wonder at it."

"I have no doubt my mother would have every awareness as to why I am so frustrated." Edward lifted his head and raked one hand through his hair. "She seems so very determined to thrust Miss Williams at me that I do not know what I am to do. I do not understand it. I have never shown any inclination towards the lady."

"Your mother is set on her, however?" As Edward

nodded, Lord Hammersmith shrugged. "Perhaps the young lady has expressed an interest in you."

Edward threw up his hands. "*Every* young lady has expressed an interest in me," he answered, speaking not with any pride, but rather with an awareness that this was how things stood. "Almost every young lady here has, at some point, attempted to catch my attention... all the unmarried ones, at least."

Lord Hammersmith smirked. "And by 'almost every young lady', you refer to Miss Moir, do you not?" His grin grew all the more as Edward turned his gaze steadfastly away. "Do not think I have not heard some of the things she has said to you – and you to her, in fact. I watched as she accidentally flung a snowball in your face. I am surprised you did not hear me laugh, for the sound of my mirth was so great, it echoed across the gardens towards you."

Edward turned sharply, his face flushing with embarrassment. "I was not at my best," he admitted a little curtly. "I was rather taken aback by the shock of having a massive snowball flung in my face."

"Which is quite understandable," Lord Hammersmith replied. "Although I did see that Miss Moir was not willing to meekly accept your harsh response. She spoke quite openly back towards you. I would have thought such a sharp response from the lady would have turned you away from her, but instead you appear to be eager for her company, given how frequently you watch her."

Edward turned to his friend, a frown dotting across his forehead. "And you seem to have been watching me much more than I was aware of."

"I am your friend. I notice when you are changeable."

Taking a breath, Edward looked away again. "You are

mistaken, however, regardless of your observations. I have no particular interest in Miss Moir."

"Then why do you appear to be so concerned with the lady? What is it you are thinking of when you look at her?"

Letting out a heavy sigh which he hoped would push his friend's questions away, Edward groaned inwardly. Given how Lord Hammersmith's eyebrows only lifted, his grin growing, it seemed he would not be willing to step away from the conversation as yet.

"Very well." Spreading his hands, he lifted one shoulder. "It was the 21st of December yesterday."

"Yes, of course. St Thomas' Day." Lord Hammersmith nodded in understanding. "I left a list of instructions with my staff to make certain the poor were taken care of during my absence."

The shame on Edward's shoulders redoubled itself, pushing him down as he ran one hand over his eyes, his chest suddenly constricting.

"You did not make any such provisions?"

The astonishment in Lord Hammersmith's voice made Edward turn to him swiftly. "Of course I did. However, I had just finished another conversation with my mother – one where, again, she continually urged Miss Williams towards me and I pushed her back in return – and in my anger, came storming from the parlor towards the front of the house. I saw three widows at the door, widows who had come earlier in the day. Rather than speak kindly to them, to listen to their situation, I allowed my anger and my frustration, which was directed towards my mother, to come out upon them. I cannot tell you how ashamed I am of my behavior. It was most unjust, and it is certainly not a representation of the man I hope to be. But alas, Miss Moir was present also and overheard me speak in such a despicable manner."

"Then what are your intentions?"

"I have no intentions." Edward shrugged both shoulders.

"That is nonsense," his friend retorted sharply. "I am well aware of the sort of gentleman you are. If you have done wrong, if you have judged unfairly, then you will wish to do whatever you can to make it right."

At this, Edward nodded slowly, his gaze once more going to Miss Moir, quietly grateful his friend knew such a thing about him. "You asked me what I am considering when I looked at the lady." Murmuring quietly, he gestured to her for a moment. "Well, there is your answer."

"I do not understand."

Edward chewed on the edge of his lip for a moment. "I did wrong – yes, to those three widowed women, but also in speaking to Miss Moir in the dark, foul temper I was in at the time. So my question is now, how am I to make amends?"

Lord Hammersmith nodded slowly.

"It is very strange," Edward continued, the tightness in his chest beginning to loosen as he spoke honestly. "We have been at odds of late, beginning from the summer Season."

"Why?" Lord Hammersmith frowned. "What happened?"

A little embarrassed, Edward cleared his throat. "It sounds very foolish to say aloud, but I was irritated when she refused to stand up with me. I did not ask her directly, but instead of being eager to dance with me, she suggested I step out with her friend."

"And you were displeased with her response?"

Spreading his hands, Edward nodded. "Foolishness, is it not?" Closing his eyes, he ran one hand across his forehead. "There is something about her that draws me in, something I cannot yet comprehend, but it is there, nonetheless. I find her both infuriating and fascinating in equal measure."

Lord Hammersmith swung himself around so he now faced Edward rather than looking across the room to where Miss Moir now sat. "If that is the case, then might I ask why you seem so eager to make amends? Why should you care what she thinks of you?"

Edward could give no answer. *That* was the conundrum, he realized, for there was the confusion over why he wished very much for her approval, when at the same time told himself he had no desire for her company. Or was it merely he was attempting to push her away because of the feelings she arose in him?

His mind went back to the briefest of kisses they had shared at the ball, back when he had thought to be provocative and teasing, desirous of her embarrassed reaction so he might feel himself triumphant again after her rebuffing of him during the summer Season. He had felt no such thing. There had been no sense of victory, no delight, but when their lips had touched, it had been as though a fire had erupted and swallowed them both whole. He could not understand it, not even now, but, as he considered, Edward became aware of the slow growing desire for that exchange to take place all over again. How often did his gaze drop to her lips without him even being fully aware of it? And how much of his desire to make amends now came from a steadfast hope he might be close with her in such a way again?

He drew in a sharp breath. Such realizations were very concerning indeed.

"You have gone very quiet, Your Grace." There was no

mockery in Lord Hammersmith's tone, mayhap realizing how confused Edward was at present. "My advice to you would be to pause. Do not allow your present guilt to push you into a hasty course of action. You do not wish to do anything that would jeopardize your acquaintance with the lady."

"Any more than I already have," Edward remarked dully. "I understand what you are saying. Believe me. I have no intention of acting hastily. At this present moment, Lord Hammersmith, I have no knowledge as to how to act at all!"

~

"Good evening, Miss Moir."

She glanced over at him, then folded her arms across her chest, turning her head a little away. "Good evening, Your Grace." Those words were muttered so quietly, Edward could barely hear them. His heart seemed to fall to the floor in the most miserable, downcast fashion.

"Might you be willing to take a turn about the room with me?"

Her head twisted to his so quickly, it gave him an indication of her astonishment. "Around the room?"

"Yes, I should like to speak with you, if I may. The other guests are all busy with their own conversations and I should like to have one such conversation with you also. I have not had much opportunity since last evening."

Her eyebrows lifted gently. "And what if I do not wish to speak with you, Your Grace?"

Edward swallowed. He ought to have expected such a thing from her, but still, her quick response still sent fire to burn through his chest.

"You speak very openly, Miss Moir." He had not meant

such a declaration to spill from his mouth, but now the words were spoken, he could not take them back. Miss Moir's eyes flashed, her mouth drawing into a thin line.

"I am well aware of my particular honesty, Your Grace." The edge of a smile tilted her lips. "I do not consider it a bad trait, however."

One thing. "Nor I, of course." Pausing for a moment, he rubbed at his chin, seeing her slightly narrowed blue eyes. "What I mean to say is that it is a little less expected from young ladies such as yourself."

Her lip curled. "While your words may be true, I assume a gentleman of your standing would be all the less inclined to hearing such truth from the lips of a young lady. No doubt most of them fawn over you and would never even *think* of speaking in the way I have. But I am inclined to always speak of what I feel and think, Your Grace, whether the person I am speaking to is a Baron or a Duke."

Edward went hot all over, not sure what to make of the lady. Miss Moir was the most perplexing young lady, with her character one of strength and determination. He did not think he had ever come across a lady like her. "All the same, I should be grateful to you if you would give me an opportunity."

"An opportunity for what?" Her eyes were like icy pools. "Do you not think you have done enough already? I have a fair impression of your character now, I think."

"And what would you say if I stated you do not?"

Miss Moir lifted her chin a notch, her gaze now a little sharper, assessing him. "Then, Your Grace," she began, her voice a little softer. "I would state I am uncertain as to whether I should believe you."

Without another word, she turned on her heel and walked away from him, leaving Edward to stand alone, watching her exit the room. His shoulders dropped, his heart sinking low. Miss Moir's dislike of him, her unfavorable outlook of his character, was almost more than he could bear, deeply afraid this lingering impression would be the last one she would have of his character. He could not understand why such a thing meant so much to him, but try as he might, the desire to improve her impression of him lingered there, nonetheless. He took a half step forward, stumbling after her, only to pull himself straight. No, he could not go chasing after her. Not only would he make a fool of himself, but he would be pursuing an unwise endeavor. There was nothing to gain in pursuing her, not when she was so very obviously against him. What could he do but attempt to consider what he ought to do next? When he had a plan, *then* he would pursue Miss Moir, just as Lord Hammersmith had suggested. For the moment, however, it seemed he and Miss Moir would be at odds.

"I DO so like a game of sardines."

Edward resisted the urge to roll his eyes. He had not played a game of sardines since he was a child and was a little uncertain as to playing it now. If he agreed to join in, then he might be cloistered amongst the young ladies for some time, and whilst most gentlemen would delight in this, Edward was a little uncertain, particularly if Miss Williams was to find him first! It had been a little unfortunate for Miss Moir that she had been the one chosen to go and hide herself first of all, for she had been hidden at the very back of the room and to Edward's mind, clearly unwilling to play the game. But yet his mother had spied her, and thus she was now the one secreted somewhere in the house.

"I am sure you all understand the game, since many of you will have played it as children," Lady Meyrick continued, gesturing to everyone as she moved around in a circle. "Miss Moir is hidden somewhere in this house and should you discover her, then you must also hide *with* her. Given there are so many of us, it will not take long for a large crowd to form but it will be the last of us to find Miss Moir who will face the consequence – although mayhap the shame of being the very last will be enough of a punishment!"

The room rang with laughter and Edward, despite his concern, found himself smiling. Yes, he considered, it *would* be highly embarrassing to be the only one wandering around the manor house in search of the rest of the guests. His stomach did a sudden little flip, hoping now *he* would not be last, especially given this was to be played within his own house.

"I would remind you all, you are to look for Miss Moir on your own." Lady Meyrick threw up her hands in mock frustration. "But no doubt, some of you will simply ignore such an instruction! I can see that Miss Williams and Lord Whitaker have already come to stand together. Perhaps they seek to walk in search of Miss Moir in aid of one another?"

Edward looked with interest towards Miss Williams, finding himself rather relieved she was standing with another gentleman. Perhaps this might, at last, put her from his mother's mind.

"That is all I have to say to you." Clapping her hands, Lady Meyrick opened her arms wide. "Go and find Miss Moir."

Edward held himself back, waiting for everyone to move out of the room. Many of the young ladies hurried forward to the door, eager to get out to search through the vast house. The older gentlemen and ladies had already taken themselves to the private parlor, unwilling to take part in whatever game it was at Lady Meyrick had planned this afternoon. Edward waited to go to the door as the last couple stepped through it, only for a footman to hurry towards him, having sidestepped the guests.

"A notice arrived, Your Grace, from 'Silvers' in the town."

"From the pawnbroker?" Edward looked at the footman for a moment as he nodded and then accepted the note from the fellow. Why would the proprietor be writing to him, as master of the house? It was most unusual, for any difficulties with orders or the like would be given to the housekeeper or the butler.

Edward unfolded the note, read over the three short lines, and allowed a frown to settle over his features.

'*Your Grace, an item has been given me for which I have paid an excellent price. I inquired as to where it had come from and was surprised to hear it was from your house. I am aware it was St Thomas' Day and perhaps such an item was truly given to those in need, in which case, I apologize for my note.*'

Blinking, Edward read over the few lines once more before folding the note up. "Send word to 'Silvers' that yes, I did give various items away during St Thomas' Day," he stated, as the footman nodded. "I may come and speak with him at some point, but he should not be overly concerned."

When the footman left, Edward pocketed the note and turned to wander towards the window, the dreary winter's day greeting him. The sky was a heavy grey, but as yet, no more snow had fallen. Edward felt sure it would come very soon.

"I wonder what item it is the man is speaking of." Murmuring aloud to himself, Edward tried to shrug the note's contents away from his mind, but it still lingered. The item had obviously caught the proprietor's attention – should it not now ought to catch his?

"I *shall* go and see it for myself." Nodding with a slow determination, he turned to go and join with the other guests, only for a quiet sneeze to catch his attention. His eyebrows shot so high, they reached towards his hairline. "Miss Moir, that cannot be you, surely?"

No sound came, no answer given, and Edward allowed himself a broad grin. "It is an ingenious idea," he continued, wandering towards the closed drapes on the other side of the room – drapes he could not be certain had been closed a few minutes earlier. "To hide in the very room where everyone else was standing in preparation – that will ensure you cannot be found for a long time indeed."

"Well, that was the idea." Miss Moir's cool voice came from behind the drapes and as Edward pulled one back, he was met by her icy gaze.

"I assure you it was quite unintentional that I lingered in this room," he told her, quickly. "I received a note about an item which has been offered to a pawnbroker in the nearby town. If I had not received the note, then I would have quit the room as everyone else has done."

Miss Moir blinked rapidly, and after a few seconds her face began to fill with color. "An item?"

Edward shrugged, putting her high color down to his nearness... and their seclusion. "It is of no consequence." Coming to stand beside her, he looked down at Miss Moir. "But now it seems I am to ensconce myself with you until we are found by someone else. How lucky I am, for I will not have to search through the house as everyone else has done." He stood closer than perhaps he was required to, one eyebrow lifting when she turned her head away. "And of course, because I get to spend a little more time in your company, which is always favorable."

This last remark was said with a mere murmur, and the color in Miss Moir's face heightened, her cheeks now scarlet even though she did not look at him. Moments passed in silence and still, Miss Moir said nothing. Edward cleared his throat, turning his head in the opposite direction and wondering whether or not he dared say anything about what had happened previously. The desire to speak of it was deep, beginning to bubble up within him again. Taking a breath, he twisted his head back around to her, just as Miss Moir did the very same. Their eyes met and her mouth shifted into a circle of surprise, his breath fiercely burning in his chest as their nearness became all the more evident. In an instant, everything he wanted to say was quite gone from him. All he could do was battle against the urge to drop his head.

Miss Moir was the first to look away. "Your Grace, I – "

"Wait a moment, Miss Moir." Speaking with great haste, Edward moved a little closer still, her breath touching his cheek as his hand reached out, brushing her fingers with his. "There is, as you know, something I wish to speak of. I – "

"Yes, of course. This strange note and the item which has been found in the town."

Edward's hopes shattered immediately. Clearly, Miss Moir did not want to speak with him about what had taken place. Her abrupt interruption had demanded his silence, and thus, he closed his mouth and shook his head, dropping his chin to his chest. His fingers lingered, however. They held tight to Miss Moir's for a brief moment before slowly dropping away – just as a small, shuddering breath escaped from Miss Moir.

"You were saying?" Miss Moir did not look at him but again spoke into the silence, pulling him away from what *he* had wanted so dearly to share. Heaving a great sigh, Edward began to tell Miss Moir all, choosing inwardly to accept what she had asked of him, and therefore speak nothing of the three widows had come to his door and of his own disastrous behavior in light of their request. Perhaps there was time coming when she would be willing to listen to him, but now was clearly not that time. He would have to wait until she was ready, if ever such a time came.

CHAPTER SIX

*A*ugusta did not think her heart had ever beaten so furiously. The Duke of Meyrick was looking back at her with a calmness which she simply could not match, for her own fears were burning so furiously, it was a struggle to hide them from him. He was telling her of an item which had been taken to the pawnbrokers, an item the proprietor wanted to make certain the Duke was aware, although as yet, the Duke did not appear to have any knowledge as to what the item was specifically.

That was something of a relief.

Augusta blinked as the Duke continued on with his explanations, her mind searing with guilt as she recalled how, in a moment of foolish temper, she had plucked the china figure from his side table. She had acted in a fool-hardy manner and now the consequences were soon to follow up on her, of course. The Duke was stating how he intended to make his way to the pawnbroker's establish-ment to see this item for himself – what would he say when he realized it *was* his? The Duke had the resources to easily discover where it had come from. The three widows would be spoken to and no doubt, they would tell him of Augusta's actions, leaving her utterly ashamed.

Still, no one had come to join them as they played a game of sardines as the Duke finished, and Augusta did not know where to look. She had thought herself quite clever, choosing to slip back into the room once everyone else had gone in search of her. She had seen the Duke, but he had not seen her, and it's only been when she had been unable to hold back her sneeze, he had realized she was there. Their nearness to each other was building a great many feelings within her, but her guilt weighed them all down very heavily indeed.

"A pawnbroker's shop in the town has this item, you say," she murmured, as the Duke nodded. "How interesting."

"I should hate to think one of my servants has taken something of mine and used it to pay for some financial difficulty or other." The Duke grimaced, his brows dropping low. "I do not want to believe that any of my staff could have done such a thing, however. My servants are all very loyal and if there was some trouble, I am certain my house-keeper or the butler would be able to deal with it."

A great fear began to push itself up, looming over Augusta as she gazed back into the Duke's eyes, seeing the shadows which now clouded his green eyes. Her stomach dropped to the floor, her blood beginning to writhe. She should not have touched a single thing in the Duke's study. Anger had driven her to it, but anger was no excuse, for she ought to have been able to control herself, to look at her actions with calmness rather than act with stupidity.

At least the three widows will have something to keep them through the winter.

"I am sure your servants would never dream of doing

such a thing. It will be something you have given yourself. You did say there were many who came to your door on St Thomas' Day, did you not?"

The Duke gave her a small, sad smile, and for a moment, Augusta's heart twisted sharply, afraid he might begin an explanation as to what had taken place when she had come upon him. But instead, he only sighed, nodded and looked away, allowing her to breathe a little more easily.

"Perhaps it is a mistake. Something that was said to be yours but was from another manor house. I am sure there were other houses who would have given items and coins to the poor."

"Certainly they would have. Perhaps you are right."

She could not look at him; her shame burning too strong for her to lift her eyes to his. She feared he would see something in her eyes and would realize there was more to her questions than she was giving away at present. She could not even bring herself to turn her head in the Duke's direction. How great a mistake she had made! Her anger and her upset has been the driving forces behind her foolishness and now she had taken something that had not been hers to take. It had been hidden at the back of a small table, behind several other items, and thus she had decided the Duke did not require it but now, however, she understood her actions tied her tight with guilt and shame – guilt, she feared she would never be able to rid herself from.

"You have gone very quiet, Miss Moir."

Attempting to force a smile, Augusta looked in his direction, still aware of how close he was to her. "We are playing a game of sardines, Your Grace. I believe we are meant to be quiet."

This brought a jovial laugh from him, and in that moment, something shifted between them. Augusta did not know exactly what it was, but her heart seemed to turn over, revealing itself afresh. The Duke's attitude to those three widows had horrified her, yes. He had reacted poorly, but should she not give him the benefit of the doubt and allow him, at the very least, to explain what had happened? It was what he wished to do, was it not? Twice, he had attempted to speak with her, and this circumstance has been his third opportunity – and still she had rebuffed him.

But I can never tell him what I have done. If he tells me of his guilt, will I not be obliged to tell him of my own?

The shame stuck her words to her lips, and she turned her head away once more. How could she ask him to explain himself when she herself held so much guilt of her own?

"I know I have ruined myself in your eyes." As though he had known what she was thinking, the Duke began to speak, his words open and honest and burning through Augusta's heart. "I have tried and I have failed to explain myself to you twice. You do not wish me to speak with you as yet, and therefore, in respect, I will not demand you listen to me. I will not beg you to hear my explanations. But when you are ready, Miss Moir – if you are ever ready, then I would be grateful indeed if you would hear what I have to say."

Augusta kept quiet, doing nothing other than look back up at him. The softness in his eyes spoke of honesty, and Augusta's own heart gentled in return. Desperately, she tried to remind herself of the moment she had seen him losing his temper with those three widowed women but, for whatever reason, it did not seem to pain her so very much. Perhaps it was because of the fact she recognized her own mistake, her own foolishness, her own folly. Yes, the Duke might want to tell her of what he had done and ask for her forgiveness, but would she not have then feel her own noose of guilt tighten? Would she not have to tell him the truth in return? And how poorly would he think of her once he had learned the truth?

Her eyes closed and Augusta pressed one hand to them, hiding her expression from the Duke. Why should she consider what the Duke thought of her? She had never let such considerations be part of her thinking before. Her emotions spiraled like a ribbon in the wind, desperately seeking somewhere to tie itself but finding no anchor.

"Miss Moir?" The gentle concern in the Duke of Meyrick's voice had Augusta looking towards him again. Her heart ached, desperate to allow him to speak, to explain himself so they might draw closer – but she could not allow herself to do so, not when her conscience would demand the same truthfulness from her.

"Miss Moir." His voice grew quiet, his closeness to her increasing with every moment as Augusta held his gaze, aware of the moment his fingers touched hers. The burning ran all across her skin, going from her fingers to her very heart, smoke billowing through her heart. This gentleman was doing nothing but confusing her; her conflicting emotions were driving her from one consideration to the next until she did not know what it was she was even *trying* to think. Everything within her seemed to be pushing her closer to him, her desire now for his fingers to twine with hers – and even for him to clasp her to his heart. For what was the second time, Augusta fought to bring back the memory of the Duke shouting at the three widowed women, attempting to rid herself of the desire steadily growing, but the image would not come. When his other hand sought hers, she did not resist, she did not pull away, even though the sensible thing to do was to react with such force that the

Duke was would then apologize for his forwardness. Again, she tried to find her concern for his character, her disgust at his behavior, only for another memory to take its place entirely. It was as if they were standing together under the kissing bough, his hand tight in hers, his lips so brief and yet so sweet. Without being aware of it, Augusta let out a shuddering breath, recalling how he had clasped her so tightly when they had danced, his strength evident in his careful yet firm hold. She had no danger of being swept away – but was she in danger of being overwhelmed now? Unable to move away from him, Augusta tilted her head back just a little, still gazing up into his eyes. The only sound she could hear was her own heartbeat, becoming faster and faster the longer she looked up into his face.

"Miss Moir." The Duke's voice was slow and soft as he spoke her name for the third time. Instead of pulling away, instead of moving back, he shifted his feet until they were a little closer... and it was no longer just their fingers that touched.

"If you are going to hide, you shall have to do a good deal better than this! I heard you speak Miss Moir's name quite clearly."

With a great exclamation, the drapes were pushed back and Augusta practically fell back against the wall as the Duke twisted away from her, forcing a quick smile to her lips as Miss Hastings discovered them.

"Yes, yes, you have found us. We grew a little bored, hiding so quietly, and thus we decided to begin to converse – which appears to have been our downfall!" The Duke was ready with his answer as Augusta looked down at the floor, trying desperately to regain her composure. Had Miss Hastings not interrupted, then what would have happened between herself and the Duke? She could not understand her own mind but was aware of how much she wished to know him, the desire to fling herself into his arms. She wished to continue from where they had been forced to break apart, her desire to do so was almost impossible to ignore, and she was struggling to keep her composure. Her breathing was still quick, her heart still pounding, and, as Miss Hastings came to ensconce herself with them, Augusta forced herself to breathe steadily, closing her eyes and forcing her thoughts from her mind.

"I am afraid you will have to move over a little more." Miss Hastings giggled as the Duke came to stand closer to Augusta. His shoulder brushed hers, his hand running down her arm to press lightly at her fingers for a moment before they stole away again. Catching her breath, Augusta twisted her head and looked up at him, seeing his eyes suddenly dark as he looked back at her, his jaw tight. They would be very close together very soon, she realized, for as more and more people find them, the space would become crushed and she would end up pressed tight against the Duke. For many young ladies, that would be most wonderful thing indeed, but for Augusta at this present moment, she found herself both afraid and confused over the closeness they would soon share again.

As Miss Hastings talked for the three of them, Augusta pulled her gaze away and concentrated on quietening her heart into a slower, steady rhythm – but still her mind tormented her. How could she desire such a nearness to the Duke of Meyrick when she had always told herself there was no desire for a closeness between herself and such a gentleman? She had always pushed the very idea away, standing alone from the other young ladies of the *ton*... only now to find herself present amongst them. The Duke was beginning to push himself into her heart, but Augusta was afraid to permit him entry. Her confusion and doubts grew with every second that passed, knowing there lay a choice in the path before her. If they were to draw nearer to him, then the closeness she thought of, the intimacy she desired, only had a hope of fulfillment *if* she told him the truth. Would she have the bravery and the courage to tell the Duke the truth about what she had done with his precious figurine?

"You cannot be thinking of going into the town. I know it is near to the Duke's manor house but look at the weather! It is already beginning to snow and the flakes are huge and are coming down very quickly indeed. It is too much of a risk."

"And yet, I think I would quite like the short drive into the town, Mama." Giving her mother a quick smile, Augusta turned away so as to hide the slight tremor that ran through her frame, desperately praying her mother would not decide to come with her in order to keep her safe. "Lady Rebecca and her mother are determined to take a short drive there, and I would like to join them. After all, if it *is* to snow a great deal, then it would be best for us to step into the town today for fear we will not manage to do so otherwise."

"Lady Rebecca is going with you?"

Augusta nodded. Lady Rebecca was a friend but as yet, Augusta had not told her about the figurine and what she had done with it, feeling far too much shame to unburden herself, even to her friend. When Lady Wilbram, Lady Rebecca's mother had indicated she herself would be taking a short drive into the town with her daughter, Augusta had quickly asked if she might join them, stating she had never been into the town and would simply like to see it before the house party came to an end. Lady Wilbram had been more than happy to permit her, and thus it had been decided. Augusta's sole intention, however, was to step away from Lady Rebecca for only a few minutes as they meandered through the town, in the hope she might discern which shop held the Duke's china figure. If she were lucky enough to find it, then she would make certain to do whatever she could to get it back. She could either place it back in the study where she had found it without saying a word.... Or confess the truth to the Duke before returning it. As yet, Augusta was not certain as to which she would do.

"I did hear the Duke of Meyrick state the milliners was very fine," her mother murmured, as Augusta glanced back at her. "Are you looking for new ribbons or the like?"

"I may make a small purchase." Her heart began to beat a little more quickly as her mother nodded slowly, her gaze shifting as though she were considering joining them. "Did not the Duke suggest the entire company make our way to town? If he thinks it safe, then I am sure he is correct."

Augusta licked her lips. "Yes, Mama, but many of the guests have chosen to stay indoors. It shall not be a long trip."

Her mother nodded slowly, her lips pursing. "I had thought to join you but another look out of the window has convinced me to remain here – and I do think you would be better off staying at the manor house also. The snow is coming down very heavily."

"I shall be quite all right, Mama." Filled with utter relief, Augusta swept from the room, giving her mother any further opportunities to either consider joining her or to argue over Augusta's determination to depart. The last thing she required at this moment was for her mother to hold her back. Of course, Lady Sutton could not know why Augusta was so eager to make her way into town, but the eagerness was now growing into desperation, as her eyes caught another flurry of snow at the window. This might be her only opportunity to get back the figurine with a diamond set at its heart, growing concerned as to what might happen should it linger in the shop any longer. It was unlikely, but someone else might take note of it, and thereafter choose to purchase it for themselves.

Within a few minutes, Augusta found herself ensconced in the carriage with Lady Rebecca on one side and Lady Wilburn on the other. Much to her relief, no one else decided to come with them at the last moment and when the carriage pulled away, Augusta's shoulders dropped and her eyes closed in gentle relief.

"It is snowing still." Lady Wilbram's voice held a note of concern. "I do hope we will be quite safe."

"I am certain we shall, Mama." Lady Rebecca's reassurance spread like warmth through the carriage and Augusta smiled back at her friend, allowing herself to relax entirely. Within a few moments, however, Augusta found her thoughts turning to the Duke once more. When they had been pressed tight together during the game of sardines, how eager she had been to move into his arms, despite the fact she had been greatly upset over his previous behavior. How could such a thing be? The man was nothing but infuriating, and yet her heart longed for him. This was a man who had appalled her with his callousness but yet who now wished to explain himself to her – and, most likely, to apologize. His attempts thus far had been brief and broken due to her unwillingness to listen, although Augusta had to confess to herself that she considered such attempts sincere. Would she truly hold his behavior against him, especially if he sought now to apologize and to make amends? Could she truly be so cruel?

Silently, Augusta began to question as to why the Duke had been so harsh to those three widows. His response to them had not been one of gentleness but it was not as though he had not been generous to them already. He *had* already aided them, but they had come again. Their explanation had been reasonable and to her mind, the only response to their plight should have been generosity of spirit, given they had offered their coins to those who could not leave their small dwelling places. Did he now regret behaving so?

"You appear a little lost in thought!" Lady Rebecca gave her a small smile. "Are you quite well? It is not like you to be so silent."

"I am quite well." She smiled at her friend. "I am glad to see you are happy."

"I am." Lady Rebecca smiled softly. "I hope, one day, you shall be as happy as I am also."

"I do not think I will ever be as happy as you." A broken, sorrowful laugh shattered the otherwise quiet carriage. "I do not think I deserve it." This last sentence was spoken in a half whisper as Augusta turned her head to look out of the window. What she had done in taking the figurine and giving it to those three women still hung heavily on her shoulders. Lady Rebecca immediately began to pronounce to Augusta there certainly *would* be a gentleman who would make her so but Augusta could only nod. She did not think happiness of that kind was for her, not until she had remedied what she had done... and even then, the guilt might still linger. The thought of telling the Duke of Meyrick what had taken place was a tight knot tying itself around her neck, one which tightened every time she thought of his face. Would he spurn her once he learned the truth? Would her heart be utterly broken?

Much to Augusta's relief, they soon reached the town. It was rather quiet, with one or two townsfolks nearby, going from shop to shop. For a few moments, Augusta simply looked around her. With the gently falling snow, the town appeared very picturesque. A gentle smile graced her lips as Lady Rebecca and her mother exclaimed the very same things.

And then her gaze landed on the sign for the pawn-broker and her smile immediately fell. It was a small building at the end of a long row of shops, with painted blue doors cracked and peeling with the weather. One side was a little ajar. Did that mean the shop was open?

"I-I think I shall take a small stroll around the market square." Waving her hand vaguely in the direction of the pawnbrokers, she smiled briefly. "I will be only a few minutes."

"Do you have any shop you intend to step into?" Lady Rebecca asked, as her mother murmured something about the cold. "I can come to find you, if you wish."

Augusta grasped her friend's hand for a moment. "Do not trouble yourself. You are to go to the milliners, yes? I will step in with you after only a few minutes."

"Very well." The town was small enough for Augusta not to become lost or to battle any difficulty. Parting ways, Augusta wandered slowly around the market square, slowly making her way towards the pawnbrokers. She glanced around the square once more, only to see Lady Rebecca waving one hand, about to step into the milliner's shop. Returning it with a smile, Augusta waited for the door to close behind her friend, only to then hurry towards the pawnbroker and step inside.

The air was dusty and dank, making Augusta shiver lightly as the cold nipped at her fingertips. By some strange happening, it appeared to be colder in the shop than outside, and there was little by way of light. The shop was so filled with items, barely any daylight came in. A single candle burned on the desk at the far end of the shop and Augusta moved quickly towards it.

"Is anyone here?" Her hands curled at the quiver in her voice. "Hello?"

Something creaked and Augusta started in surprise as a voice eked out of the darkness.

"Good afternoon."

Pressing one hand to her heart, Augusta swallowed hard as a small, wizened gentleman came out from the shadows to sit at the chair by the desk. His eyes glinted behind half-moon spectacles, and it took her a few seconds to compose herself. She could not simply come out and ask him for the particular figurine, for then she would give herself away – and what if the Duke came to this particular shop thereafter?

"Can I help you?"

Augusta took in a breath. "I thought I would look for a small gift." She spread her hands, trying to smile despite the panicked beating of her heart. "At Christmas time, I do like to furnish my friends and family with small gifts if I can. I have bought nothing for my mother, as yet." That was true, at least, and Augusta's heart pushed back against the threatening guilt.

The man rose from his spindly wooden chair. He was a good deal shorter than Rebecca, with a somewhat scruffy beard and a bald head which glinted in the candlelight. However, when he smiled at her, his whole expression lit up. "I am certain we can find you something special."

Rubbing his hands together, he tipped his head. "Is there anything you have in mind? I have many things in this shop."

Augusta smiled back at him. "I can see that. It is a marvelous establishment, I must say."

The man inclined his head in a bow as Augusta thought quickly, trying to make sure she could suggest something which would then lead him to offer her the figurine without being too obvious. She did not want to lie nor add to her guilt and thus chose her words carefully.

"I do like small figurines." Looking around, she saw a miniature bloodhound and a small boy figurine sitting on a small table to her right and moving to them, she picked both up. The items were not the same as the Duke's but it certainly would give the man an idea of what she was seeking.

"Things like this?" The man took the figures from her and Augusta nodded.

"Yes, like these. Do you have any more? I would like to purchase a few." Augusta winced inwardly, fast, demanding her features remain in a pleasant expression. Yes, she was hoping to find the figurine she had given to the three widows, but at the same time, thought she might purchase something to give to her mother on Christmas Day. Could she not do both, even though her motivations for being in this shop were entirely askew?

"I do have a few other items." Turning his head and looking over his shoulder, he beckoned her back towards the desk. "Should you like to see them?"

Augusta's heart slammed against her ribs. Putting as much brightness into her voice as she could, she voiced her request and smiled. With a brief nod, the man stepped away for a moment, only to return with four boxes stacked one on top of the other. He opened every box and set out the four china figures.... but much to Augusta's horror, each china figure had a diamond at their heart. One was of a young girl, one of a young lady, another of a lady with some flowers and the fourth, a gentleman doffing his hat. Augusta knew she had not given the three widowed women the gentlemen china figure – but as to the other three, she could not remember which it had been.

Seeing the man lift his eyebrow, Augusta demanded she smile. "These are beautiful." Going from one to the other, she tried frantically to recall which one she had taken from the house, but nothing came to mind.

She took a breath.

"I should like to purchase them all."

The man's smile slowly faded. "All of them?"

Augusta nodded. "Certainly – and the bloodhound and small boy figures also. The bill can be sent to my father, Viscount Sutton, and he will pay it in full upon receipt."

The man blinked. "I see." His smile slowly began to return. "I am very grateful, but I can't give them to you as they are. The boxes are very dusty and the figurines must be cleaned. I can send them to where you are staying?"

Augusta shook her head. "I shall take them now. Pray, do not concern yourself."

After a moment, the man shrugged and handed the boxes to her. Augusta was able to balance them carefully, with one hand under the bottom two and the other two wedged against her side so that she held them in the crook of her elbow. No doubt her cloak would be rather dirty when she returned to the manor house, but it could not be helped.

"The bill?"

Nodding, she opened her mouth to give the address of

her father, only to pause for a moment. "I must ask you to keep my purchase quite secret." She managed another smile. "My mother will be very pleased with them, but I should not want her to know of my purchase before Christmas Day."

"Of course." The proprietor smiled kindly and again, guilt seeped into Augusta's heart. She was speaking so just to cover her own actions – and her shame grew even greater.

Augusta gave the man the address of her father, knowing he would not care what she had purchased. Once the sale was completed, she made her way out of the shop and back quickly towards the carriage. Handing the tiger her purchases, she then made to go in search of Lady Rebecca at the milliners, only for the shop door to open, and the Duke of Meyrick to step out.

"Miss Moir." Smiling, he inclined his head as though he had been expecting to see her. "Lady Rebecca said you had taken a short walk around the town but I could not seem to find you."

Nodding, Augusta struggled to find a satisfactory answer to the Duke's statement, only to be saved from her requirement to respond by the arrival of the Lady Rebecca and her mother, their arms laden with purchases. Immediately, the Duke sprang to action, helping them with their items back to the carriage.

"You are returning to the house, are you not, Your Grace?" Casting a glance towards the now heavy skies, Lady Wilburn shook her head. "The snow has stopped for a moment but I am sure it will return again."

The Duke of Meyrick smiled as he helped Augusta into the carriage. "I think I shall remain here for a little while longer. I will return to the house soon enough."

Augusta swallowed hard, her skin prickling as she

turned her head away. What if he was to go to the pawnbrokers? What if he were to find out what she had done?

"I do not think that wise." Lady Wilburn shook her head again, ignoring Lady Rebecca's murmur to hold her advice back. "I myself am very unsettled at the thought of the carriage driving back along the roads. The snow has been so very heavy and I think– ah-ha!"

As though the skies had heard her, it immediately began to snow again and the Duke's forehead caught with a frown.

"It seems the snow is growing heavier." His frown deepened as he glanced at the skies and then back to Lady Wilburn. "If you would prefer it, Lady Wilburn, if it would comfort you, then I would be very glad to accompany you back to the house. I assure you, we will be quite safe, but all the same, I shall ride alongside you until we are safely ensconced within."

Augusta drew in a slow breath as Lady Wilburn exclaimed her relief and gratitude. Her eyes darted to him, catching his gaze for a moment and all too aware of the fierce reaction that burned within her when their eyes met. His gentlemanly behavior towards Lady Wilburn was appreciated – and yet so at odds with how he had spoken to those three widowed women. Her conflicting feelings tore pieces out of her heart as she dropped her head, far too aware of the purchases she had made now sitting beside her in the carriage. If only she had not taken the figurine in the first place, then she would be able to listen to his explanation and his apology without hesitation or fear. And yet, she had acted impulsively and now would have to decide whether or not she told him of her actions. Was there any possibility that, after his apology to her, she might give her apology to him? And who was to say what would happen thereafter?

He might turn from me and never look back.

The possibility sent a heaviness into her heart which seemed to drag it to the ground. Settling back into her seat, she kept her gaze to her clasped hands, unable to look at the Duke any longer. She sat quietly as the carriage pulled away, desiring no questions nor conversation from any party. But all the while, her heart sent question upon question to her, every moment of the drive back to the house.

CHAPTER SEVEN

*I*t was a little frustrating to Edward that he had not been able to visit the pawn shop but given he had a responsibility to his guests, Edward had been obliged to ride alongside the carriage to make sure the lady felt comforted. It also meant he had been able to see Miss Moir from his position in the saddle and had indeed been aware of her glancing towards him now and again. It has only been the briefest of looks, but it had come on more than one occasion. Whether such glances meant anything, Edward could not say, but all the same, he had been grateful for them. It meant at least Miss Moir was not going to ignore him. Perhaps there might be hope of her listening to his explanations in due course.

"I am relieved you came home when you did." His mother walked into his study yet again without invitation and settled one hand on his arm. "The snow has been falling very heavily these last few hours."

Edward nodded in agreement. It was only as he had ridden home that the snow had begun to fall a good deal more heavily than he had anticipated. Lady Wilburn had announced herself all the more relieved he had joined them and, were he truthful, Edward had been glad he had chosen to return with them also. Had he lingered in town, it might have been all the more difficult to return through such a snowstorm.

"I have noticed you are a little melancholy these last few days." Lady Meyrick turned her gaze towards him, her eyebrows lifting gently. "I am a little concerned for you, I confess."

Edward offered her a brief smile. "That is generous of you, Mother. I will admit to being a little... distracted."

He did not give any explanation and his mother lifted one eyebrow, waiting but Edward merely shook his head. He had no intention of going into further explanations. Lady Meyrick frowned and opened her mouth... only to close it again, giving him a small shake of her head.

"I am the cause of your distress and I am sorry for it." She squeezed his arm lightly, then made to step away. "Oh, I did think to ask you about this evening's entertainment. A Christmas play, is it not?"

Edward nodded, looking over at her. "Very good, I believe the players have already arrived."

Edward held his breath, waiting for some suggestion that he sat next to Miss Williams. Much to his surprise, however, his mother simply offered him a smile and then took herself directly to the door of his study.

"Mother."

She paused, her hand on the doorknob, turning her head around to look at him.

"I- I am grateful to you for this house party."

Seeing her look of surprise, he spread his hands. "I am aware I have been ungrateful. I have complained and moaned and given all manner of excuses as to why such a thing would not be a good idea. I have attempted *not* to enjoy myself, first pretending your parlor games do not interest me, but the truth is, Mother, I have found this a very pleasing endeavor. The winter can be so very dreary, and I am glad to have had entertainment and company."

Lady Meyrick took a moment, studying him and perhaps fearful he was teasing her. But then there came such a beautiful smile on his mother's face that Edward's heart grew a little bigger. He realized now how upset his mother had been over his complaints about the house party. Yes, he had been irritated over her lack of consideration and yes, she certainly ought to have discussed all manner of things with him beforehand, but that did not mean the house party itself was not a pleasant one. Indeed, it was more pleasant than anything he had expected.

"Thank you for saying such things to me. It means a great deal." His mother smiled at him for a moment longer and then closed the door behind her, leaving Edward quite alone.

"I should have been a good deal more grateful." As if he needed to berate himself a little more, Edward spoke aloud, meandering to look out of the window. He ought to have been more considerate of all the effort his mother had made from the very beginning. Had she not done so, then this winter might have been a very dull one indeed and he might have spent it almost entirely alone – and what was that thought in comparison to what he had now had? Weeks full of guests, laughter, entertainment and a great deal of delight.

With Christmas only a few days away, Edward's heart lifted all the more at the thought of getting to spend it with Miss Moir. Yes, there was still a good deal they had to discuss, and much he had to apologize for, but after their shared moment behind the drapes, Edward was hopeful he would not have to endure her silence for long. He could only pray that if he told her the truth, if he could be honest with her about his own feelings, then she might be willing to forgive him.

But what if she does not?

His heart lurched suddenly as he turned from the window, wandering back across his study and recalling how his fingers had taken hers. In doing so, she had not pulled her hand away. In fact, had he not held her hand for some moments? It only had been an interruption which had ended the closeness; the intensity that had been built shattering, suddenly replaced with a strange awkwardness. What was it he wanted from the lady? Chewing on the edge of his lip, Edward began to consider what it was in his heart when it came to the lady. He wanted her approval, wanted her to see his regret, his desire to charge, was eager for her to desire his company. He wanted her to desire... him.

The thought was so startling, Edward caught his breath, coming to a standstill. Both he and Miss Moir had been at odds at first and, at the start of the house party, had found himself wanting to tease her in return for her rebuffing of him during the summer season. But that wish had changed into something new, something much more profound. The thought of her leaving his house at the end of the house party felt painful. The astonishment which now befell him at such a realization had him passing one hand over his forehead, feeling sweat beading there. It was more than he had ever imagined he could feel. To accept his feelings were more severe than he had ever imagined was truly altering.

Capturing his breath, Edward set his shoulders. These feelings would have to be considered carefully before he acted on any of them. He had never allowed himself to consider matrimony before, so why should he do so now?

"Because I have never had such feelings before." The answer was all too clear, and as Edward spoke those words, his heart lurched all over again. He had never had such feelings for any young lady, had never found himself caught by them, nor his thoughts ravaged at every spare moment considering her. So what was he to do with this sudden awareness?

"She *did* hold my hand." Murmuring to himself, Edward immediately flung his hopeful thought away from his heart. He could not let himself even imagine a future with Miss Moir, not when he had disgraced himself before her in such a horrific way. There had to first come an explanation, accompanied with the faint hope of forgiveness, and thereafter, he would have to wait to see what would follow. *Then* perhaps, then, if she forgave him, if their acquaintance was recovered, then he might allow himself the smallest bit of hope as to his affection.

His mind was suddenly pulled from thoughts of Miss Moir, as he noted something was missing. The corner table by his study door was usually filled with a variety of trinkets – trinkets he cared very little for but were there, nonetheless. The last time he had looked, all of his trinkets had been present. Another quick look told him something was gone. He frowned harder. What was it that was absent? His gaze went over and over the small group of ornaments, trying to recall which one was gone – and after a few moments, it came to him.

The small China figurine with a diamond at its heart.

His brow furrowed as he rubbed one hand over his chin. Wherever had such a thing gone? The servants would not have taken it, surely, and there was no need for it to have been moved, unless, of course, it had required cleaning. Had there been a breakage, then he would have been informed of it.

"Unless it was one of the new maids." The idea had him shaking his head. The housekeeper would have supervised the new maids for the first few days of their duties, making certain they knew what to do and what was expected. If there had been a breakage, then the housekeeper would have informed him at once. He did not even question it for a moment. *So where has it gone?*

Tucking his last question into the back of his mind for the moment, Edward forced himself to think about his present responsibilities. He had been in his study for far too long already. The guests would be waiting yet again for his company. The dinner gong was soon to sound and, as Edward quit the room, he smiled quietly to himself, recalling how he had made certain he would be sitting next to Miss Moir at the dining table. She would be to his left while he sat at the head of the table and, as he walked down the hallway, Edward realized once more, Miss Moir was at the forefront of his thoughts.

"Gentlemen, we are not free to linger over our port this evening as we usually do." Edward smiled at the murmurs of light frustration. "We are all to make our way to the ball-room to enjoy a magnificent Christmas play which will be presented for our entertainment."

"Let us go at once." His mother rose from her chair and the ladies followed suit, with the gentlemen coming in between to mix themselves in with the ladies. Edward turned to the door, his eyes on Miss Moir. She was waiting for those who were eager to hurry to the door and thus, Edward held himself back, allowing his mother to lead the way forward. He had been close to Miss Moir all through dinner and they had managed some pleasant conversation, albeit with others near to them both. Desirous to remain as close to her as he could, he did not hesitate. "Miss Moir, might you walk with me to the ballroom?"

To his very great delight, she did not hesitate, but accepted his arm at once, although no smile fell to her lips. They were the last to leave the dining room and Edward strolled rather leisurely, rather than walk with any great speed. His thought of making conversation began to burn away, his mouth suddenly going dry as he fought to know what to say. Miss Moir walked beside him, also silent, though her eyes darted up to his.

"I do hope you enjoy the evening." It was a somewhat mediocre remark, but it was better than saying nothing. "I am sure the play will be excellent."

"I am certain I shall." Her voice was quiet, lacking any sort of excitement or even anticipation for what was to come. Edward's lips twisted. No doubt she was considering what had passed between them on St Thomas' Day – and if she was considering that, then how could they ever find a way forward?

Confusion bit down hard. He longed for more with Miss Moir, willing now to admit it openly to himself. Was there any hope he could tell her more when they could not even discuss the past?

As if she somehow knew what he had been thinking, Miss Moir suddenly squeezed his arm. "I believe I must ask you to forgive me, Your Grace."

Edward's head swung around towards her. "Why must I forgive you?"

Miss Moir drew in such a long breath without saying anything that Edward's concern began to grow. "Is something wrong?"

"There is something I wish to speak with you about." Miss Moir's words began to tumble, one over the other. "I have no doubt you will be deeply dissatisfied with me, however, I –"

"Miss Moir." Quite certain he knew what she was about to say, Edward immediately began to dissuade her. "Your lack of willingness to hear my apology and my explanation for what has taken place is not something I would hold against you." He stopped walking, her eyes searching his face and her lips trembling just a little as she turned to face him, and Edward's concern grew all the more. Was she really this concerned over her lack of openness to his explanation? Was she afraid of his reaction to her delay, fearful he was some sort of tyrant, demanding she speak with him, regardless as to whether or not she was ready?

"Miss Moir, do not push yourself to listen to me. I am not angry with you for your hesitation. I am not frustrated. I am truly open to waiting until you are willing to listen to me. There is nothing for me to forgive you for in that regard."

Miss Moir's hand found his, her fingers pressing his so tightly, Edward's eyebrows lifted. Whatever was concerning the lady, it was clearly of great importance.

"You misunderstand, Your Grace." The lady drew in another deep breath, her shoulders settling. "As I have said, I am aware my explanations will bring you to think poorly of me, for I have behaved in much the same manner as you in terms of my reactionary behavior."

Edward shook his head. The lady was unburdening herself again, with no reason to do so. Had he not communicated himself clearly? Had he not made it quite plain he did not think badly of her for being a little less than willing to listen to his explanations?

"There is no fault in your hesitation. Your reaction to my anger is more than understandable." His other hand found hers also, and they stood together, much as they had done behind the drapes. "I should not like to hear another word as regards this, Miss Moir. When you are ready, I will explain myself to you, whether it be today, tomorrow, or even in the summer Season." As he spoke, something pushed him closer, and Edward responded at once, aware there was no one else in the hallway save for the two of them. There was some impropriety, yes, but it did not seem to enter his mind at the present moment. All he could see was Miss Moir, his gaze on her lips, her eyes still shining with concern. How much he wanted to remove that from her!

"No, Your Grace, I – "

"I believe there will be more than one explanation I must give you, Miss Moir – when the time is right, of course." The words were spoken with a great deal of meaning playing through them, and in an instant, Miss Moir's cheeks flushed, her head twisting slightly away – but her hands did not pull from his. Was it possible she felt the very same as he? Was her own heart softening towards him despite all the confusion and hurt the last few days of their acquaintance has brought?

Her eyes closed for a moment. "I think you misunderstand me, Your Grace."

Edward did not know what she meant, her actions quite at odds with his words. She spoke of misunderstanding, but her fingers twined through his, and her gaze slowly drew back towards him as he allowed himself to watch her.

The smallest of smiles edged from the corner of her mouth and Edward was lost. The sweetness of her was overpowering. His throat grew tight and he swallowed hard, aware of just how much feeling he held in his heart for Miss Moir, and yet how uncertain and unsure he seemed to be at present also. There were so many things they had not discussed and thus, it was not settled between them. However, this growing affection simply would not allow them to stay far apart. Did Miss Moir feel the very same uncertainty as he? Was she drawn to him too, despite a heart filled with uncertainty? What could he offer her but the truth? Could he not tell her of his heart, in the hope she might respond with the same honesty? Had so much to explain – how her closeness made him want to be the very best of gentlemen and how his past behavior made him all the more mortified.

However, he said nothing.

Silence flooded the space between them as Miss Moir continued to look up into his face, her fingers still tight through his. It was as though she were waiting for him to respond, to take the first step in an action that would change their future. With a heart beating fiercely with anticipation, Edward slowly began to lower his head in response. Miss Moir tipped hers back.

"Your Grace?" Sharp footsteps on the hallway floor and the sound of his name being called sent Edward flying back. He pushed himself as far apart from Miss Moir as he could only to then scuttle back towards her and offer his arm recalling they had been meant to have been walking together. She accepted it without a word, just as Lord Ossington came around the corner.

"Forgive me, Your Grace." Clearing his throat, the gentleman looked away, as though realizing he had stumbled onto an important moment. "Lady Meyrick has sent me."

He gave no further explanation and Edward sighed to himself, fully aware of exactly what his mother had done. She had sent Lord Ossington in search of him, perhaps becoming a little frustrated at his tardiness.

"I think, Your Grace, I require a few moments." Miss Moir threw a glance to him, then pulled her hand away. "Please do not wait on my account. I will join you all in a few minutes."

Edward could only nod, desperate to speak, desperate to explain to Miss Moir of what he felt, to talk about what had almost happened and how much he desired a connection of importance between them... but such things could not be communicated by only a look. Thus, he offered her a smile, which she briefly responded to before turning on her heel and walking away from them.

"I do apologize for interrupting you."

Edward shrugged one shoulder as he turned to walk towards the ballroom alongside Lord Ossington. "It is not your doing, and it was not deliberately done."

"No, indeed it was not. In fact, had I known you required a private conversation with Miss Moir, I never would have interrupted you."

Edward looked to his friend." I do hope I can count on your discretion."

"Yes, of course." Lord Ossington put one hand to his heart. "I will not say a single word. I highly doubt any of the guests will notice Miss Moir's absence or her return."

Edward offered a grateful smile. "Thank you." Walking into the ballroom, Edward was immediately pulled into his responsibilities, even though his heart was still burdened over what had almost taken place with Miss Moir. Yet again, they had been so close to something and still so far from it. He would need to speak to her again, would need to make his desires clear, and tell just how much he was beginning to care for her – and how sorry he was for the mistakes he'd made thus far. Edward's only prayer was she would be willing, at the very least, to consider him, for he did not think he would be able to endure without her.

CHAPTER EIGHT

I almost kissed the Duke.

The thought that twirled around Augusta's mind had her eyes closing. Sometimes she was glad of what had taken place, but other times she was horrified over how close she had come. When the Duke of Meyrick had lowered his head, she had forgotten about her attempts to apologize. Her intention had been to tell him of the figurine and of what she had done, despite the fact that she had been exceedingly anxious over doing so. As they had walked along the hallway, she had been suddenly desperate to tell him everything, to let him know of her guilt and to beg of him to forgive her. To her mind, it had been the only way they might ever have a chance of happiness. But he had mistaken her intent, and she had not the strength to fight him, not when his closeness had stolen everything else away. In that moment, it had been as though nothing else mattered and her desire for his lips to press to hers had begun to burn furiously. When they had been interrupted, when she had stepped away, her embarrassment had swirled with shame. Shame she had not spoken to him honestly, that she had not determined to be entirely clear before any further closeness could take place.

I am relieved that nothing of significance took place.

Pressing her lips together, Augusta closed her eyes for a second, considering. Had the Duke kissed her, then she would be in an even greater predicament. She was resolved, however, that she would tell him the truth one way or the other. It was not, as he thought, that she did not want to hear his apology over how he had spoken to the widowed women, but rather she had desired to unburden herself. If only he had listened to her, then things might have changed between them already... although not necessarily for the better, she acknowledged.

"I do not think you have heard a word I have said."

Augusta kept her eyes on her embroidery, embarrassed. She and Lady Rebecca had a quiet parlor all to themselves and Lady Rebecca had been speaking for some minutes, but Augusta realized she could not repeat a single word her friend had spoken.

"Are you quite well?" There was no anger in Lady Rebecca's voice, only a soft concern.

"I am very well." Giving her friend a brief smile, Augusta turned her attention back to the embroidery, trying to push the incident with the Duke from her mind. "Forgive me. I was concentrating hard and did not hear you speak." That was true, at least – although she had not been thinking of her embroidery.

Lady Rebecca touched her arm, her eyes searching. "Your embroidery cannot be that difficult, surely?"

Augusta tried to smile but instead, a sigh came from her lips. "I find it a little trying," she admitted, fully aware that it was not of the embroidery she truly spoke, but rather the

Duke. "Sometimes there are so many knots that I struggle to untangle it all."

Lady Rebecca tilted her head, saying nothing.

Sighing, Augusta shrugged her shoulders. "You understand what I mean, I think?"

"I surmise we do not speak of embroidery." Lady Rebecca smiled gently, her gaze still rather intense. "What is the matter, my dear friend? This is a season for joy and happiness but I see you more melancholy than anything else."

Setting her embroidery aside, Augusta let out another sigh. "I do hate to be so. I am sorry if I my despondency has weighed you down."

"It has not affected me not at all." Clearly now a little concerned, Lady Rebecca shifted so she sat on the edge of her chair. "Whatever is wrong, I beg of you to share it with me if it would be an aid to you."

Augusta hesitated. Lady Rebecca had endured her fair share of confusion but now such things had come to an end, Augusta was free to share her own difficulties. "I fear you will think me very foolish."

"Mayhap I shall." Lady Rebecca smiled gently. "If you wish to tell me you find yourself drawn to the Duke of Meyrick, then I can promise you it will not be as surprise."

A ball of heat began to roll around Augusta's stomach as she dropped her gaze.

"You are embarrassed." Lady Rebecca shook her head. "I did not mean to make you so."

Her face flaming, Augusta tried to find something to say but instead ended up shrugging helplessly. What Lady Rebecca had said was part of her difficulty, yes, but it was not all of it. Certainly, she *was* drawn to the Duke and clearly, she could not hide such a thing from her friend. "I have been attempting to keep this from everyone.... Perhaps even from myself also."

"But it is quite reasonable to have such feelings." Lady Rebecca shrugged. "I do not think poorly of you at all."

"But I am foolish, am I not?" Her heart beginning to thump with uncertainty, Augusta looked over at her friend, desperate to hear her judgement. "I have always told people I would not be drawn to a gentleman simply because of his standing.... and now that is precisely what I am doing!"

"But you are not going to him *because* of his standing, so therefore, you are not foolish." Lady Rebecca smiled gently. "Come now, allow yourself to feel such things without hesitation. You need not be overly concerned."

"But I have always told myself to stay away from him. Even during the summer season, I have always had very little interest in the Duke, refusing to fawn over him simply because of his standing in society rather than because of his character."

"Does that mean that the Duke's character is a poor one?"

The quiet question drove into Augusta's soul. No, she considered silently. The Duke's character was not something she considered to be a poor one, despite his previous behavior. Certainly, there was to be an explanation for what he had done and she was sure he wished to apologize, but she had seen other sides to him also, observing things she could not ignore. His willingness to assist Lady Wilburn and accompany the carriage back to the house when she had expressed her concern over the snow had been honorable, as well as his constant consideration of his guests. All of those things counted for something.

"That is a question that I shall leave with you, I think." Lady Rebecca smiled gently as Augusta continued to contemplate. "But I do want you to understand that your feelings are not something to be embarrassed about. They should be joy knowing that the gentleman clearly returns your feelings."

At this remark, Augusta thrust herself to her feet and began to stride around the room in great discontent. "I cannot be certain of that." Her words rubbed hard against the memory of how he had held her close only the previous evening, and at these words, Lady Rebecca merely shook her head.

"I think you know as well as I that you can be *very* certain of his feelings."

Letting out a slow breath, Augusta stopped pacing and turned to her friend again. "But he does not know the truth." At this remark, Lady Rebecca's smile slipped in obvious confusion, having very little understanding as to what Augusta meant.

"There are parts of my character and some of my behavior of which I am greatly ashamed." Swallowing, Augusta looked away from her friend." If the Duke of Meyrick were to know of it, then he would turn from me."

"Everyone has failure and shortcomings," Lady Rebecca reminded her gently. "You cannot think that yours are any worse than anyone else's. To my mind, you are a wonderful friend with a great many attributes."

"But I am also impulsive." Her heart aching, Augusta pressed her hands to her eyes "This is where my thoughts linger at present."

Her friend tilted her head, studying her. "I do not think I fully understand you. I can see there is some sort of deep sorrow within you, however. Your eyes betray it. If there is something that you wish to speak of exactly, then I would be glad to listen. I will not judge you, not in any way."

Augusta nodded. It was as though her pain were bubbling up within her, forcing the words towards her lips - and she was unable to hold them back, whether she wished to or not.

"There was an incident with three widowed women on St Thomas' Day." With a small sigh, she spread her hands. "He was angry about what was being asked of him. I did not understand it, for as I said, it was St Thomas' Day, and therefore a day when great generosity of spirit is offered."

"And which is expected also." Lady Rebecca nodded slowly. "Thus far, I agree with you."

Augusta flung out both hands. "You have not heard the worst of my story. I overheard the Duke dismissing these women in the most unfortunate manner. He had, I realized, already offered them a good many coins, but they in turn had gone to give it to those who were unable to remove themselves from their homes."

At this, Lady Rebecca's expression softened, one hand going to her heart. "How much need they must be in."

"That was my feeling exactly, so you can imagine my horror to hear him so dismissively."

"Of course I can." Lady Rebecca frowned. "Did he give any reason as to why he was speaking so harshly?"

Augusta shook her head. "Not as yet. However, the Duke has asked for an opportunity to speak with me, to explain himself and no doubt, to apologize. I have not yet given him a chance, however."

A small frown flickered across her friend's forehead. "Is there any reason why you have not?"

"At first it was because I was overwhelmed by his behavior, so upset by it that I thought I never wished to be in his company again. But now..." She trailed off, dropping her head forward. "There is more to my reasons for delay – entirely selfish ones, I might add."

Lady Rebecca said nothing, waiting for Augusta to continue her explanation. Finding it rather difficult to be so honest about what she had done, Augusta took in a deep breath and then, after another moment, began. "In my fury of temper, I stated I would go to fetch some coins from my room for these three widowed women, given that the Duke of Meyrick had stated he had finished with the matter," she began. "However I...." Her eyes closed as shame pushed through her heart. "However, on my return to the three ladies, I passed by the study and –"

"So this is where you are hiding!" The door was pushed open, and just as Augusta was about to begin her explanations, her mother stepped into the parlor. "I have been looking all over for you. Lady Meyrick is gathering the young ladies to finish with the Christmas decorations for tomorrow." She looked expectantly from Lady Rebecca to Augusta and back again." You are intending to take part, I hope?"

Augusta let out a slow breath, wishing her mother had given her only a few more minutes of privacy with Lady Rebecca. Her friend appeared to be of the same mind, for she returned Lady Sutton's request with a short, rather wry smile, and with a quiet breath, rose to her feet

"I would be glad to join. Thank you for coming in search of us."

With a small sigh of frustration, Augusta followed after her friend and her mother, ignoring the slightly questioning look on her mother's face. Somehow, Lady Sutton was aware Augusta had been talking of something important.

"Come along then, come along." Lady Sutton ushered them both out of room as Augusta linked arms with her friend, standing aside to allow her mother to then lead the way.

"You will be able to tell me the rest of your conundrum later."

Sighing again, Augusta lifted one shoulder. "I do hope so." With her mother now striding before them, Augusta allowed herself a small shake of her head. "Matters with the Duke of Meyrick are so very confusing. He is very handsome, of course, but with all that has taken place, I find myself deeply confused and yet, at the same time, drawn to him."

"I am sure it will all become clear to you soon."

"Mayhap it will." Augusta tutted in frustration over her own lack of self-control. "I cannot seem to remove the Duke of Meyrick from my thoughts. No matter where I go, he is always there. I cannot seem to take my mind from him."

A small sound from behind her caught her attention and turning her head, Augusta's breath hitched as she saw none other than the Duke walking only a short distance behind them. She had kept her voice low as she was speaking with Lady Rebecca, but had he overheard her? Her whole body seemed to burn with a furious, unquenchable fire as her gaze caught his for just a moment. The returning small smile and the light in his eyes seemed to say he had overheard every single word she'd said.

"Your Grace." Her strangled voice warned Lady Rebecca he was near as she twisted her head back around, his deep voice followed after her.

"Good evening, Miss Moir."

Augusta did not think she could even glance in the Duke's direction for the remainder of the day, such was her embarrassment. The words she had spoken to Lady Rebecca began to run over and over in her mind. It was utterly mortifying to think the words she had spoken had been overheard by the Duke himself! He would have heard her speak of his confusion, have listened as she spoke of how desperately she could not get him from her mind, how overwhelmed by his presence. Would he be glad to hear such a thing from her? Would he be relieved to hear that she had such feelings? Or would he be a little frustrated she felt so much confusion?

~

"Good evening, Your Grace."

It was a cold but clear night. After dinner and refreshments, a few of the guests had thought to step outside for a very brief stroll under the moonlit sky. The snow still lay on the ground, hardened by the frost but the paths had been cleared and thus, Augusta was able to walk without concern. She had been quite contented walking without company, but the Duke of Meyrick had stopped to wait for her – even though Augusta had found herself burning all over again by a single look in his direction.

"Might I offer my arm? It is a little precarious."

Swallowing at the tension in her throat, Augusta accepted it, appreciating his offer of support. They began to follow after the other guests but, try as she might, Augusta could not think of what to say to him.

"You were very quiet this evening, Miss Moir." His gaze travelled to hers. "You did not appear to be much in the mood for charades."

Augusta smiled despite the flood of tension. "No, I did not wish to take part, Your Grace, although I think those who did join in found a great deal of enjoyment." She gave no explanation for her lack of participation but instead tried to smile. "You appeared to enjoy yourself a good deal, however." If she were honest, she would tell him that she had smiled a great deal at the game, enjoying observing but not taking part. The Duke himself had been very funny indeed. He had gesticulated so wildly that the entire company had been in flurries of laughter.

"Yes, I do fancy myself a bit of a showman at times," the Duke acknowledged. "I do not seem to be embarrassed by my behavior on such occasions - whereas I confess, there are a great many times where I have made such a fool of myself that I cannot help but feel shame at it."

A faint smile lingered on Augusta's face, all too aware of what the Duke was speaking of. She wanted very much to talk to him honestly, but it required such courage from within her – and after she had failed the last time, it seemed to take an even greater length of time to build.

"We have all done things where we are greatly embarrassed by our behavior." Remarking softly, she kept her gaze low, not able to look at him as he led her forward along the path with the rest of the guests now a good few strides ahead of them both.

"But I am certain that you have never behaved in such a cruel fashion as I have done." Stopping, he turned to face her as her hand slid from his arm. "Might you be willing to listen to me now, Miss Moir?"

Swallowing hard, Augusta nodded. "But only if you are willing to listen to me thereafter, Your Grace." Her voice choked out from between her lips, and the Duke nodded quickly, seemingly very little concerned, as though he did not think there would be anything of significance nor severity in what she had to say.

"Yes, of course." He took a moment, looking from her face to the ground and back again. "I do hope that you understand how highly mortified I am by my behavior towards those three widows." His breath blew out like a soft cloud, his features illuminated by the moonlight. "What you will not be aware of, however, is the fact my mother has been pushing me towards one particular lady. On St Thomas' Day, I had only just come from a meeting with her where I again demanded she dropped the subject, only for her to insist once more that she believes the lady to be the very best consideration for my future."

Augusta's stomach suddenly lurched at the thought of the Duke pursuing another young lady.

"I do not believe her to be the right choice." The Duke shrugged, looking away. "My mother, however, has been insistent. Throughout this entire house party, she has been pushing me towards one particular lady, although I do not yet understand why. She pretended she was not so also, which infuriated me all the more. Therefore, I came from that particular argument to the front of my house to see three widows that I had *already* spoken with and given coins to earlier that day."

Nodding, Augusta licked her lips, listening to the Duke and finding herself barely aware of the cold.

"I did not behave well, Miss Moir." The Duke let out a long breath. "I was so fueled with anger and frustration that I took it out on the three widows - people who ought to deserve nothing but kindness from me. Your sharp words were well deserved, for everything you said was correct. Looking back upon myself, when I hear my voice saying those words to them, when I think about how I dismissed them from my sight, you cannot know the shame that weighs so heavily upon me. I made a mistake, Miss Moir. It is not one that I am likely to repeat, for I assure you I do not have such a fierceness of temper but was twisted up with frustration – not that such a thing is an excuse! Given how fiercely you expressed your discontent and how candid you were with me, I feel so ashamed of my actions. I *should* have a heart filled with nothing but compassion for those less fortunate than myself, regardless of my own circumstances. I can only apologize to you for the horror of what you witnessed from me – and I can assure you, I will do all that I can to apologize to those I injured and continue on with making certain they are taken care of during the winter time."

He held out one hand to her, waiting for her either to take it or to step to one side. Augusta could choose to take his hand in acceptance of his explanation and of his apology, or she could ignore it and thus make her continued dissatisfaction quite clear.

"One final thing." The Duke's voice was as steady as his gaze. "I want you to know I have made arrangements with my staff for a great platter of food to be sent to each and every household within my estate on Christmas Day. Everyone within this vicinity shall have something more from me – and it is a gesture I intend to continue every year, Miss Moir. This, I confess, is all down to you and your frankness. You have nothing to apologize for in that regard, for I am, in fact, grateful to you for every word you said to me. It was what I needed."

Augusta let out a breath she had not known she had been holding, her eyes brimming with sudden tears. The Duke had spoken like a gentleman, acknowledging his mistake, asking for her forgiveness, and not shirking from his responsibilities. A lesser gentleman might have refused to acknowledge it altogether and certainly would not have permitted her to make any comment on his behavior. But the Duke was not such a man. Instead, he stood tall and accepted his responsibilities and mistakes – and had shown his appreciation for her.

Without delay, she reached out and took his hand. The Duke let out such a breath of relief that Augusta was surprised at just how much her acceptance of him meant.

"We all have times where we have failed." Augusta managed to smile back, her shoulders lifting a little. "I am very glad to hear of your generosity, Your Grace. I am sure many people will be more than grateful."

"I should always seek to do more than just what is required," the Duke told her clearly. "You were right to state how much I have and how little they have. I have more than I shall ever require and those who come to ask - whether it be the second time or the twentieth time – ought to be given as much as I can." The Duke squeezed her hand. "I assure you, Miss Moir, my aim is to be so generous of both heart and spirit, not only at Christmas time but also throughout the year."

A joy tore at her heart, not over her own actions, but those of the Duke's. He *had* listened to what she had said, even though her words had been cutting. Rather than push them aside, he had chosen to act upon them.

"You are remarkable, Miss Moir." The Duke moved a little closer, his expression lit by the light of the full moon, and Augusta's frame was filled with such an intensity, even the cold air seemed to dissipate. "I understand your desire to contemplate things before you listened to my apology and my explanation. I am grateful to you now for even considering what I have to say."

A wedge of guilt broke through her happiness and Augusta shuddered violently. The Duke dropped her hand, perhaps mistaking her shiver being from the cold, only to draw her into his embrace. His actions had her heart laughing and crying at the same time. Should she not use this opportunity to tell him everything? She did not want their closeness to grow even more before she had told him what she had done with his figurine.

"We have had moments like this often, have we not?"

The Duke's low voice wrapped around her as she settled her hands lightly against his chest, her head resting on his shoulder as the desire to speak began to fade, though she fought to keep it close. Her longing to be back in his arms had been growing steadily and now to have the fulfilment of such desire was exhilarating.

"Yes, Your Grace. We have." Keeping her face exactly where it was, Augusta fought against the wish to look up, a little uncertain as to what would happen if she did so.

"There have been times when I wished to continue our conversation – our moments – only to be interrupted." The huskiness of his voice had Augusta closing her eyes, knowing exactly what it was she wanted and yet too afraid to seek it. She could not allow herself such a freedom, not when she had her burden to share with him. To act rashly would be foolishness.

"It does not seem as though we are to be interrupted now, however."

His words rang through the cold air as her heart beat hard against her ribs, aware of exactly what he was offering her and all the more yearning to accept it.

She drew in a shaking breath.

"I cannot." Regret burned through every pore as she finally gave in to the urge to lift her head just a little, her eyes catching his before she began to pull them away. "There is more that I must say," she continued, leaning out of his arms despite the desperation to remain. "You have spoken to me and I believe I requested that you listen to me also."

The Duke frowned, his eyes grey in the moonlight. "If you wish to apologize again for having me wait to speak with you, then I would beg of you not to do so."

Augusta shook her head. "It is not that." Trying to find a way to begin, she swallowed once, stepped back again to settle some distance between them, and looked up. "I have also behaved in a manner that is unfitting, Your Grace. You have made your mistakes. I have made mine. You have apologized for yours and now I must do the very same. An explanation is required and thereafter, I will beg of you to forgive me."

Augusta shivered lightly, clasping her hands in front of her, her head dropping as she scoured her mind for the right words to begin. "I have no doubt that you will be angry with me indeed, but I am willing to accept that. I have been so very confused and I simply cannot allow us to become closer if - "

"You put too much of a burden upon yourself." Before Augusta could finish, the Duke's hand caught her wrist, his fingers running to find hers once more. "If you are confused over what you feel at present, then do not fear to tell me so. It is perfectly understandable to be in such a conundrum. Even recently, I found myself in such a difficulty, although I confess my feelings become clearer with every moment I spend with you."

Aware now he had heard her speak to Lady Rebecca, Augusta pressed her lips together. That was to what he referred *and* what he thought she was trying to say. Yes, her feelings were a little confused but it was not she wanted to say to him. For the second time, he had unwittingly attempted to dissuade her from her honesty.

"Yes, Your Grace." Augusta squeezed his hand, trying to determine how to speak honestly and without hesitation. "I will not pretend I do not know as to what you refer to, for it was apparent you might have overheard my conversation with Lady Rebecca." Silently thinking that it would be best to be honest from the outset, and about everything - including the state of her own heart, Augusta held out her other hand to him.

"I care for you. I find myself pulled towards you. I have spent so long determined that I would never think more highly of a Duke or a Marquess, as so many others do. I would not think such gentlemen more worthy than others, due only to his standing or his wealth. And in such regards, I have managed to do so. However, for whatever reason, our connection at this house party has grown so significantly, my heart refuses to remain unaffected. Instead, it fills with an affection for you that I never once imagined could be held within it. I admit I have never felt such feelings before, which is partly why I have the confusion I spoke of. If you are asking me, however, whether or not my heart is engaged with yours, Your Grace, then the answer would be yes."

He smiled at her. "How glad I am to hear that, Miss Moir." The gentleness of his words had her cheeks flushing and she looked away, just as the sound of laughter rang towards them, alerting them to the returning of the other guests. "Again, it seems, we are to be interrupted, but I hope our conversation can continue again *very* soon. There is more, I think, that I require to express."

The slight coyness of his smile had her breath hitching as she struggled to respond. The Duke of Meyrick was no longer just a gentleman of her acquaintance, nor someone she had begun to notice – but instead, the only gentleman who had ever truly taken a hold of her heart.

CHAPTER NINE

*E*dward smiled to himself as Miss Moir entered the room. Her eyes seemed to find his almost at once, only for her face to pink a little as she dropped her gaze away. Her smile, however, was unable to be hidden. It was fixed there for everyone to see, although her head lowered so no one would suspect the reason for it. Edward had no doubt it was meant for him only, however; given all they had shared together the previous evening.

He had never meant to pull her so close and in such an inappropriate fashion, but the way she had spoken had made him desperate to reveal his heart and thus, he had been unable to stop from enfolding her into his arms. How willingly she had gone into his embrace! She had sighed and softened, her hands at his chest, her head on his shoulder. Edward did not think he had ever felt anything so exhilarating. It was not the first lady he had held tight, of course, but there was something about Miss Moir that affected his heart, in a way no one else had ever done before. He could not seem to breathe without her. His mind full of her, his every spare second thinking of her. Regardless of the day or the time or the occasion, the only person he wanted near to him was Miss Moir... and this Christmas seemed all the more special because of her.

In fact, I think I should like all my Christmases with her.

The thought was an astounding one, and Edward found himself dragging in a breath, trying desperately to recover from the significance of it. To accept such a thought would be to consider what he wanted when it came to the lady and the idea weighed heavily on his mind. To think about the future would mean to think of Miss Moir, for one did not seem to work without the other. After this house party, he realized, his frown beginning to grow, Miss Moir would leave his house alongside her mother, and he would be left without her anywhere near to him. She would return to her father's estate and he would remain here. The next time he saw her, it might be during the summer season! He could not imagine so many days without laying eyes upon her or to be in her company. To experience such closeness, such delight, was one thing, but to think of being apart from her was quite another. "And I do not wish to think of it." Realizing he had muttered aloud, Edward looked around the room, praying no one had overheard him. Much to his relief, no one looked in his direction and Edward let out a slow breath. These feelings were confusing but not unwelcome and he certainly did not want his friends to know of it. He did not think any of them were paying the least bit of attention to him at present, however. Their minds were much too full of Christmas Day and all it would bring. The Yule Log had already been brought in, thanks to Lady Lavinia and Lord Blackhall, the greenery was present throughout the house and a fresh joy seemed to fill everyone within the house. Would Christmas Day itself not give him an opportunity to tell Miss Moir precisely how he felt? But to do so,

Edward recognized, he had to sort through them before such a time, so he knew precisely what he wanted to say.

And what if she returns my feelings?

"They will be one final parlor game this evening!"

Before he could allow his thoughts to linger on Miss Moir any longer, Lady Meyrick got to her feet, and the rather exuberant crowd of guests let out small whoops and cheers. Edward grinned at the sight of his mother's faint blush, all too aware of how much she had enjoyed herself. These last few days, she had not mentioned Miss Williams once either, and Edward was highly relieved, hoping now the matter was at an end. She still would not tell him *why* she had pressed Miss Williams upon him so heavily, but Edward considered that he did not need to know. So long as the lady herself had no expectations – and his mother also - then nothing more needed to be said.

"I should like you all to think of the very best gift you can bring the Duke, this Christmas," Lady Meyrick began as a slight murmur of amusement came from the assembled guests. "I have no doubt many of you will think of something most particular, something which will please my son, but mayhap, you might also think to bring him something which will give some mirth. He will decide which is the most suitable, the most desired, and which is to be returned to the giver."

Edward sat up a little straighter, looking at his mother, but she would not catch his gaze. She had not told him of this game, had not let him know in advance – but mayhap it was the point. Perhaps she had not *wanted* him to be prepared, so it would be just as much fun for him as it was for the guests. Edward glanced around the room, seeing many of his friends grinning. No doubt they had something ridiculous in mind with which to bring him. There would be a good deal of merriment, Edward supposed, and that was precisely what Christmas Eve was for.

"We may bring anything we wish?" The grinning face of Lord Ossington caught Edward's attention, and he rolled his eyes at his friend, seeing the man grin. "Anything we think would be pleasing to Your Grace?"

Edward caught the glint in Lord Ossington's eye and immediately his stomach twisted a little. Whatever was Lord Ossington planning?

"Certainly." Lady Meyrick waved a hand. "You have but a few minutes, however. Be off with you!"

Those who were playing immediately leaped to their feet, with some hurrying from the room on hasty feet. Miss Moir did not move, however, clearly intending simply to sit and watch what took place. Edward did not mind in the least, for it meant he could sit and watch her in much the same way as she would watch the proceedings. Again, their eyes met, and again, they shared a smile, with Edward's heart leaping so high it felt as though it were stealing his breath to disguise. He had never met anyone as lovely, as beautiful, as kind-hearted nor as forward as Miss Moir. Her character was something he now admired rather than finding frustrating. Her willingness to speak honestly was a trait to be recognized and held in high admiration, for Miss Moir did not hide her true self away. She did not pretend. Indeed, she had spoken of her heart with such frankness, he had been unable to stand quietly, forced to respond in a way that had drawn them together so they could no longer be parted. Yes, there was much to discuss and certainly Edward had to consider what it was he sought from his ongoing acquaintance with the lady, but one thing was for certain. He wanted Miss Moir to be a steadfast part of his future.

"And here they are come back." Lady Meyrick smiled broadly as she held her hands out to the first guest to return. Lord Ossington came to join the mounting throng also, although Edward noted silently he had not actually left the room. After a few minutes, the guests formed a long line and Lord Ossington stood at the back, sending Edward's anxiety rising a little higher.

Lady Meyrick gestured to the first of them. "Now everyone has arrived, each of you may present your gifts to the Duke one after the other, and he shall decide which is of the most worth to him."

Edward cleared his throat, feeling rather awkward as the first young lady stepped forward." I bring you a bottle of port, Your Grace."

The whole room began to chuckle as Edward accepted it from Miss Hastings.

"A worthy gift, certainly," he declared, as the murmurs of laughter and agreement reached his ears. "I am certain almost everyone here is all too aware of how much I enjoy my port."

"Mayhap a little too much on occasion," someone shouted, and again the room rang with the sound of mirth. Edward let out a slow breath, trying to relax, telling himself to enjoy what was being played out. Lord Ossington had something planned, he was sure, but no doubt it would be presented with good humor and great sincerity. This game was simply meant to entertain them all and thus far, it was doing precisely that.

"Lord Rosenthal?" Lady Meyrick directed, as the gentleman stepped forward. He held something behind his back and after a very gracious bow which made Edward chuckle, he held out a sprig of mistletoe.

"A gift which every gentleman seeks, I think," he

explained as Edward took it with a flickering frown on his forehead. "This is so you may hold it over the head of any young lady you wish, and they will be obliged to kiss you."

It took all of Edward' strength of will not to look over to where Miss Moir sat, not wishing him to make himself too obvious in front of the other guests. He could not embarrass the lady, especially when they themselves were not entirely certain as to what they felt for each other.

"What say you, Your Grace?"

Glancing at his mother, Edward spread his hands, the mistletoe still in one of them "It is an excellent gift." Setting it down beside the port, he grinned. "Though I cannot decide whether I would prefer the port or the kiss!"

The game continued for some time and everyone continued to laugh and smile as the gifts were given. Lord Ossington drew near and Edward lifted one eyebrow, seeing he was the last.

"You appear to have empty hands, Lord Ossington," Edward remarked, tilting his head.

"Ah, but I have not yet fetched my gift!" So saying Lord Ossington turned on his heel, strode directly across the room and, offering his hand to Miss Moir, then led her back towards Edward. As he did so, the entire room went still as Lord Ossington grinned, clearly unaware of the effect he was having.

"Your Grace, may I present to you the gift I believe you desire the most, this Christmas."

Miss Moir, who had been blinking in confusion, immediately closed her eyes. Rather than going scarlet, she went grey, her hand now clinging to Lord Ossington's, her fingers white on his arm. Edward did not know how to respond, seeing Lord Ossington grin, becoming aware that everyone else in the room had remained silent. What was he to do? It was clear to him that yes, Miss Moir *was* the young lady with whom he wished to spend the Christmas season with – but to state so would surely embarrass her, if not mortify her all the more than she already was? Could he not simply laugh and state that yes, he would desire a dance or a kiss from Miss Moir before the house party was out, given he had not managed to do so already.

"I thank you, Lord Ossington." Edward kept his gaze fixed on the gentleman rather than look to Miss Moir. "You are quite correct, I suppose. Miss Moir and I were not very well acquainted at the start of this house party – but I am glad to say now our acquaintance has improved. Perhaps you are right, Lord Ossington. Perhaps the greatest gift I wish for this Christmas, is to be happily acquainted with all of my guests."

At this, a rumble of approval came from the other guests, but Edward directed his gaze straight back to Lord Ossington, lifting one eyebrow gently. His friend's grin quickly began to die away, mayhap realizing he had made a grave mistake. Did the gentleman not recall he had been sworn to silence? Did he not now see that in speaking in such a way as this, he had not only embarrassed Miss Moir but had broken the promise he'd made to Edward himself? Rather irritated at this, Edward finally let his gaze rest on Miss Moir. Her face was sheet white, her eyes dropping to the floor, her hands clasped in front of her, her chin to her chest. All Edward wanted to do was go to her, to take her hands and to apologize for what had been said, but all he could do was merely hold her gaze, desperate for her eyes to lift to his, as though he might comfort her with only a look.

Lady Meyrick clapped her hands, and everyone's attention was swiftly returned to her. Edward's heart lurched as Miss Moir quickly turned on her heel and hurried back across the room, sitting down in her chair and squeezing her eyes closed.

"Your chosen winner, Your Grace?" Lady Meyrick gestured to the large array of gifts he had been offered, attempting to keep the brightness in the room. Recalling only a few of what he had been offered and his thoughts tell him still entirely centered on Miss Moir, Edward dragged in a long breath. How much he wanted to go to her! How much he wanted to apologize, even though he himself had done very little wrong.

"Your Grace?" Yet again, his mother murmured and Edward blinked, realizing he had not given her an answer as yet.

"Of course." He tried to smile. "Of course, it must be the port." His response brought only a few trickles of laughter and nothing as overwhelming as before. Lord Ossington's foolishness had ruined this entire game.

Lady Meyrick began to speak of something else they might do, another game they might play, but as Edward watched, Miss Moir took herself from her chair and, like a shadow, slipped to the door. His heart ached for her, his desire to go with her burning furiously, though he knew he could not. He would make himself much too obvious and did not want to embarrass her any further. With a heaviness weighing down his soul, he let the lady leave.

CHAPTER TEN

"Augusta."

Augusta lifted her head as her mother came into the room. "Yes?"

"Are you quite all right?"

It was late in the evening. Augusta had retired to her bedchamber some time earlier, having been overcome with mortification with what Lord Ossington had done.

"I am well, Mama."

"You may be well, but I am still concerned." Her mother came a little further into the room and sat down on the edge of the bed. "Lord Ossington's remarks were rather embarrassing for you, I imagine." She offered a small smile to Augusta, although her eyes were filled with a softness that spoke of concern. "I think Lord Ossington meant only to be mirthful."

"I am sure he did," Augusta answered with a shake of her head, "but instead he was nothing but embarrassing."

Her mother held her gaze. "Might I ask if there was any truth in what he was suggesting?"

Augusta's breath twisted in her chest. What was she to

say? As yet, nothing had been spoken of between herself and the Duke, but then again, they certainly had drawn closer as of late and had shared a great deal.

"I...I do not yet know, Mama."

Her mother's eyebrows lifted a little.

"There *may* be," Augusta admitted. "But nothing of any seriousness has been said." Reaching across, her mother squeezed her hand.

"The Duke is an honorable man. He will not do anything without intention."

Augusta smiled but said nothing, her throat suddenly constricting. There was great pain when she thought of the Duke of Meyrick, her heart filled with pain and longing. Twice now she had tried to find a way to tell him the truth about what she had done and twice she had failed. Her desire was, at present, to be honest with him even if her honesty would lead to a separation - a separation which would be entirely her own doing. However, she would accept the consequences of it regardless.

"Normally I would not advocate such things, my dear, but I know the Duke of Meyrick is in the library this evening."

Augusta's head twisted sharply towards her mother, her heart beginning to beat at a furiously rate. "Whatever do you mean?"

Her mother smiled. "Simply that."

Blinking in utter astonishment, it took Augusta a moment to catch her breath. "It would be scandalous if I were to be caught alone with the Duke, particularly so late in the evening!"

Her mother shrugged one shoulder. "Then do not get caught." Rising from the bed she smiled down at Augusta as she continued. "You have always been cautious and considered. Those characteristics will guide you well in whatever conversation you have with the Duke. I very much want your happiness, Augusta, otherwise I would not be advocating such a thing as this. But I trust you to be careful and to remain proper, for you have proven yourself to be so." Still smiling, she made her way to the door. "However, should you go, do not be too long with him, else I shall have to come in search of you myself."

Understanding this to mean her mother would look in on her again before she retired to bed, Augusta managed a small smile and a nod before her mother finally closed the door. She was almost too dumbfounded for words; had never once expected her mother to advocate visiting the gentleman alone in the middle of the night... but yet there was a trust there that she appreciated.

Her lips pressed hard together. If she did not go to speak with him now, then she might not have opportunity again. Tomorrow was Christmas Day and thereafter, the house party might soon come to an end. She would be forced to depart without any chance to speak directly to the Duke of Meyrick. Rising to her feet, she smoothed both hands down her gown, aware of the whirling nerves beginning to thread through her. Taking a breath, she lifted her chin, suddenly determined to take hold of this opportunity. Walking to the other side of the room, to the drawer where she had hidden those figurines, Augusta took them out, one after the other. Setting them down for a moment, she gazed at each one in turn, taking a slow breath. This was her only chance, to tell the Duke everything before Christmas Day... or before anything else could grow between them.

Resolved, she gathered the figurines a little clumsily and, making her way to the door, quietly stepped out into the hallway. It was dark and rather cold but she barely noticed, her thoughts set only on forcing her steps directly to the library in the hope the Duke of Meyrick would still be there.

"Your Grace." Her heart leaped into her throat as Augusta pushed open the door before stepping inside. At first there did not appear to be anybody within, but another look told her the Duke was sitting in front of the fire, his head back against the chair, his eyes closed. Was he asleep? And if he was, did she dare wake him?

Licking her lips and all too aware she was entirely alone with the gentleman, Augusta stepped fully inside the room. "Your Grace."

The second time she spoke, the Duke shifted in his chair and, after a moment, his eyes opened and he blinked rapidly, taking a few seconds to realize he was no longer alone in the room. Coming forward, Augusta set her packages on a small table and then stood next to it, her hands behind her back, her heart lingering in its furious beating.

"Miss Moir." The Duke made to rise but Augusta waved one hand.

"There is no need to get up. Please do not trouble yourself, Your Grace. I will leave if you wish it."

"Are you here to speak of Lord Ossington? I am very sorry for - "

Augusta shook her head. "No, it is not about Lord Ossington. He was being thoughtless in his attempts at mirth but it was not cruelly meant and I have forgiven him easily enough."

The Duke cleared his throat. "Then why are you here?" One eyebrow lifted, a hint of a smile on his lips but Augusta immediately looked away. She could not permit herself a single second of distraction.

"I have something I have been very eager to speak with

you about – I have tried and failed twice now and thus I had to take a hold of this opportunity."

The Duke's smile disappeared, but he said nothing, giving her the space to continue.

Augusta took in another breath, set her shoulders and looked straight back at him. "Forgive me, Your Grace. I have tried on two separate occasions to be honest. I only beg you now for a few minutes of your time. There appears to be something of significance between us and our connection is of such importance to me, I do not think I can continue without telling you everything. Judge my character, my motivations and my feelings for yourself, Your Grace, and once I have finished telling you all, mayhap you will no longer wish to be acquainted with me."

The Duke's expression instantly softened. "I am sure there is nothing you could say which would hold me back from you, Miss Moir."

Augusta tried to smile, but her lips flattened instead. "Be that as it may, I will speak to you the truth." Again, she wet her lips and tried to steady the inner shaking, taking a hold of her very soul. "I am well aware my presence here is entirely untoward but I do not think I will have another opportunity to speak with you. It must be now."

Again, the Duke made to rise but Augusta quickly held out both hands, palms out flat towards him. With a sigh and a slightly wry smile, the Duke sat back in his chair.

"Very well, Mis Moir. I swear I shall maintain my distance." When she dropped her hands, the Duke continued to smile, clearly underestimating the seriousness of what she had to say.

Taking a deep breath, Augusta gestured to the parcels. "Allow me to open these for you, Your Grace."

"If you are attempting to play the parlor game from this

evening, Miss Moir, you are a little late." The Duke chuck-led. "Although I suppose you did not bring me a gift, so mayhap I should accept these regardless."

Augusta said nothing, her fingers trembling as she unwrapped the first parcel. She could not return his smile nor his jovial manner. One by one, she opened each of the boxes and thereafter, took out the figurines one by one.

Her gaze finally lifted back to the Duke. "Do you recognize these, Your Grace?" Her voice was shaking so badly, the words would barely come. After a moment, and with his smile fading, the Duke rose to his feet and came closer. "No, I do not."

Augusta closed her eyes, her stomach roiling. "I am sure you will recognize one, Your Grace."

There came a moment of silence and then a swift intake of breath as Augusta opened her eyes.

"Wait." Reaching out, the Duke touched the third in line "I do recognize this." Frowning in obvious confusion, he picked up the small figurine. "This was missing from my study. I only noticed it a few days ago, but given the snow, I have not been able to make my way to the pawn-brokers."

Shame broke over her in a furious heat. "You need not wonder anymore, Your Grace." Augusta whispered, her eyes closing again as if she wanted to shut out the view of the Duke of Meyrick's expression. "I can assure you, the figurine is your own."

Again, silence crept through the room and, unable to bear it, Augusta eventually opened her eyes. The Duke's gaze was searching her face, no frown of anger on his features as yet as he looked again at the figurines. "I do not understand."

Sharp tears burned in her eyes as she gestured to the

figurines with a shaking hand. "I purchased these from the pawnbroker in town."

The Duke's head lifted, looking for an explanation in her features, but Augusta could say nothing. Everything was shaking, her heart seeming to burn through her skin with shame.

"You purchased these from the pawnbroker." Slowly repeating her words, the Duke rose to his full height and Augusta nodded, finding she could do nothing else. Her fingers were twisting hard into each other, the only sound the furious beating of her heart pounding in her ears. "Did you know this was mine, then?" The Duke ran one hand over his chin. "Clearly, you were aware a figurine had gone missing, although I do not recall ever speaking specifically of the item which had been taken from me."

An explanation was demanded of her. Opening and then closing her mouth, Augusta tried and failed on three occasions to explain herself.

Closing his eyes briefly for a moment, the Duke cleared his throat roughly. "That is because I did not tell you about my missing figurine. I myself was not specific."

The fact he had come to this realization all by himself made Augusta's heart drop all the more. She *had* to say something and, taking in a trembling breath, she dropped her chin to her chest.

"Indeed." Her voice was trembling, her head bowed low as she fought to find the courage to speak openly with him. "Yes, Your Grace. That is the truth. I knew you were missing the china figurine – not because you told me, but because *I* was the one who took it."

The Duke's jaw tightened, his eyes flashing. "You stole from me and then bought them from the pawnbroker in order to gain some... additional funds for yourself." It sounded more like a question rather than a statement, and Augusta quickly shook her head, tears beginning to blur her vision.

"No. I did not take them for myself. I did not bring them to the pawnbroker."

"Then what did you do?" The words were spoken with greater depth and increased fury, forcing Augusta to stifle a yelp of surprise as they echoed around her. She deserved every moment of his anger, of course. This was what she ought to expect.

Her throat tightened as she blinked rapidly, pushing away her tears. "It was on St Thomas' Day, when those three widows came to the door. I was so infuriated with your response that I acted rashly. On returning from my bedchamber – I had gone there to fetch some coins of my own - I came to your study and pushed the door open, thinking to tell you exactly what I thought of your behavior. You were not present, however, and in my frustration, I picked up something from your room which I thought would be worth a few coins. I told myself if *you* would not be generous, then I would force generosity from you." Dropping her eyes, Augusta squeezed them closed as a single tear ran down her cheek. "My anger drove me to do such a thing, although I do not say so as an excuse. I have become so aware of my guilt, have been so full of shame, it began to overwhelm me. I knew I had done wrong and thus, I went to the pawnbroker's in the hope of taking back the item and returning it to you. I could not recall which one it was and thus, I bought them all."

"And, no doubt, when I mentioned the letter I had received from the pawnbroker, your urgency only grew." There was still a hard tone to the Duke's voice and Augusta kept her eyes closed, knowing she had no strength with which to look at him.

"I battled as to whether or not to tell you about what I had done. Soon, however, I decided to tell you the truth, for I had no choice but to be honest." Her eyes opened, but she only gazed at the floor. "No doubt, I have failed in your sight, have dropped in your estimation – but I accept those consequences. After what we have shared, I could not have continued on without having you know the truth." She heaved a breath. "I was wrong and I admit I was wrong."

The Duke of Meyrick did not say a word. The heaviness around them became so oppressive, Augusta could not help but glance at him – only to regret doing so, given the dark, furious expression now melding to his handsome features.

"I am sorry, Your Grace."

A heavy sigh escaped the Duke. "So you took something which was not yours. You stole from me and gave it to those widows, feeling as though you had some right to taking on my responsibilities when I would not. Thereafter, in your shame, you went to town and purchased those figurines, intending to return the one you took once you recalled which one it was!"

Augusta nodded but said nothing. The ice in the Duke's voice only grew.

"And you say, due to our increasing... closeness, you thought it best to come and inform me about your behavior."

Swallowing at the knot in her throat, Augusta nodded slowly.

"But you only do so now, so close to the end of the house party."

Fearful the Duke would think all the worse of her,

Augusta spoke up quickly. "Pray do recall I *did* attempt to speak with you about these difficulties already, Your Grace," she managed to whisper, as the Duke shook his head. "It does not make what I have done any better and certainly does not take away from my guilt, but I wish to be quite clear my intentions have been there for some time."

"You are quite correct to say it does not detract from your guilt." The frustration in the Duke's voice was magnified by the way he screwed up his eyes, his lips pulled thin. "I never once imagined someone such as you would take something so precious from me."

"I did not think it precious." Augusta sucked in air, her eyes tight shut, knowing immediately she had said the wrong thing. "Forgive me, that is not what I meant."

The Duke had dropped his head and shoulders, rounding as his hands gripped the top of the chair. "Then please explain to me what it is you mean, Miss Moir, for thus far, all I can see is that you took something you believed to be without value to me. On top of which, and for some inexplicable reason, you then believed you ought to be able to offer it on my behalf to those who needed it the most."

Augusta found herself wanting to protest, but instead kept her mouth shut, lowering her head. There was no excuse to offer. She could make no protest, no apology she could give which would satisfy the Duke. She had done wrong, and his anger at her behavior was perfectly justified.

"You should have told me of this before we...."

The Duke trailed off and Augusta dropped her head even lower, her chin to her chest, her eyes still shut, too ashamed to look into his face.

"I did attempt to."

One glance at him stole any flicker of hope from her heart.

"Whatever you may say, you did not try hard enough." His voice was low, and Augusta's heart broke with the disdainful look he sent in her direction. "I should have known about this from the moment you regretted it."

Again, Augusta tried to find the words to say she *had* tried and had been put off by his own insistence, but the words would not come. It would not do for her to make any sort of excuse, could not lay the blame at his feet. No, it would be best simply to stand and listen, to accept whatever he said to her. She deserved all of it.

"I confess I am not only angered, but utterly shocked to hear *you* were the one who took my figurine." The Duke shook his head. "I would never have imagined you would have stolen from me." Finally, his eyes lifted to hers as she caught his gaze. "You are not the character I thought you to be, Miss Moir."

A certain desperation captured her heart and before she could stop herself, she had moved towards him, her fears growing so rapidly, she could not help but come to stand beside him, afraid now he would end their closeness.

"I made a mistake, a foolish one," she acknowledged. "But please, do not push us apart, not after everything we have shared. It has been more than I have ever experienced in my entire life, and my heart is filled with not only an interest, but an affection for you – an affection I do not think will *ever* be given to another. I think of you every day, every moment. I cannot help but have you in my thoughts and also in my heart. Please do not push me away from you, Your Grace. Might you not be willing to understand my foolishness? Foolishness, I know, is what it was. It was rash and reactionary, in much the same way as you yourself behaved to those widows when they spoke to you."

"And yet we are entirely different." The Duke stepped back from her, his eyes now a little narrowed. "I did not steal anything."

Augusta dropped her head into her hands, so close to the Duke and yet so far from him, no further than she had ever been before. "I was so afraid to tell you." Her honesty came pouring out from her, her every fear growing. "I was afraid to tell you, because I believed you would push me away, you would think me no longer worthy of your company. Is that to be our situation, Your Grace? Are you too send me away from you?"

The Duke held her gaze and Augusta's breath tied itself into her lungs, afraid to even hear the answer, and yet waiting for it, nonetheless. Silence flooded the room. No answer was given her. The Duke simply held her gaze as though she ought to be able to read in his thoughts, able to see exactly what he thought of her and their closeness at present.

"Please, I beg of you."

Aware of just how desperate she sounded, Augusta once more found herself moving close to him and this time, her hand went to his...but it was cold to her touch. No smile came to his face as he looked at her steadily and Augusta's heart tore, as though they had been pulled apart in one moment. His expression was so changed, it was as though she did not know him any longer, as though he were the Duke she had met in the summer Season: reticent and unknowable. There seemed to be nothing she could do to change it, for the Duke was the one to put the distance between them. What could she say about it? He had every right to do so, given how she had lowered herself in his eyes.

"Please." Finding herself whispering, fresh tears brimming in her eyes, she held his gaze. "Please. There must be something I can do, something I can say to change things, to improve our acquaintance again."

The Duke let out a long breath. He stood tall and, after a moment, pulled his hand away from her. He said nothing and Augusta closed her eyes, tears beginning to drip down her cheeks. His single action had shown her what he intended. There could be no reconciling, no furthering of their connection. Even though she was relieved she had been honest, the consequences of being so were nearly impossible to accept.

She turned away, blindly making her way towards the door with unsteady steps. Part of her waited for the Duke to call after her, desperate for him to call her name, to tell her it would take a few days, perhaps, but with a little time, he would understand what she had done. Instead, however, there was nothing but silence to follow after her and as Augusta made her way from the room, it was as if she were closing the door on everything that had ever grown between them.

CHAPTER ELEVEN

*E*dward stared at the figurines on the table. He could hardly believe it. How could Miss Moir have taken the figurine from him? How could she have done such a thing? Yes, the figurine meant very little to him, but it had still belonged to him - and no excuse she could give as to *why* she had done it was enough to content him.

Looking from one figurine to the next, Edward picking his own figurine up in his hand and, looking over it, shook his head. Her behavior was utterly astonishing.

"But based on my behavior."

Letting out a slow breath, Edward muttered aloud to himself, still coming to terms with what Miss Moir had told him. He understood she had been angry, yes, but how could she simply have taken something of his and given it to someone else? She had offered it to someone when there was no requirement for her to do so. Charity and generosity were *his* responsibility and his decision, whether fair or unfair, ought to be respected.

Now it seemed as though he did not truly know the lady. Yes, she had apologized, but it did not mean he fully understood her. Her character was not as he had believed it. He had thought her a little frustrating, yes, certainly determined and forthright, but he had never imagined she would have the gall to steal from him.

But she did return this to me. She told me the truth when she did not have to.

The thought was an unpleasant one and Edward threw it aside quickly. While she had indeed spent a great length of time making certain that the item was returned to him, Miss Moir had *still* been the one to take it in the first place. Her actions were the cause of his trouble at the present moment. It was too much of a shock, too much to bear to realize the lady he held a great affection for was, in fact, a good deal more duplicitous than he had ever imagined.

All of his happiness had died away in a moment. Now he felt nothing but foolishness, wondering if he had made a mistake in finding himself so in love with Miss Moir. Perhaps in keeping her current character hidden, she had done so deliberately.

The thought chased itself away from him in the very next moment, knowing Miss Moir had always shown herself to be precisely as she was. She was forthright, yes, troublesome in many ways, but she was honest at least. She had done wrong and had come to tell him of it – albeit much too late in his mind.

Edward sighed aloud and ran one hand over his chin. Despite her protests, surely Miss Moir should have told him of her mistakes as soon as she had the desire to do so? Perhaps then he might have understood her foolishness a little better, might have seen how much she regretted doing what she had in the hours or days that followed. But instead, she had clung to her guilt, had not let it escape from her. She had taken it with her, carried it through, so their continued connection might build... on the presence of lies.

His own upset abounding, Edward gripped the little figurine tightly, dropping his gaze to it. It had been a gift from his grandmother, passed down through the generations, but having very little significance to himself, for it was one of many things he had been given from previous times. It did not matter whether the figurine had any monetary value, however. The only thing that mattered was what had happened to it.

Closing his eyes, Edward tried to take a great many breaths, steadying himself, pushing away the rippling thoughts coming to his fractious mind, but still the feeling of upset and frustration grew. He ought to be able to find some sort of gladness over Miss Moir's determination to tell him the truth, had sought him out, and had done all she could to fix her mistake, but there was no happiness for him. The only thing he felt now was betrayal, to the point he did not believe his connection with the lady could be salvaged.

To his mind, there was too much damage for it ever to be repaired.

~

"It is Christmas Day!"

Edward merely grunted as his mother came sailing into the room. He had barely had a wink of sleep, thinking only of Miss Moir and what she had revealed to him. His mother's joviality, therefore, was more of a burden than anything else.

"It is a fine day, Mother," he murmured calmly, pressing a kiss to her cheek. "I wish you every blessing on this day."

"As I do to you," she replied sweetly. "Although, may I

say, you do appear a little fatigued." Her smile faded. "Your eyes are tired."

A wry smile split his features. "I am certain all of my guests will feel exactly the same way," he responded. "It is not as though many of them were early to bed last evening."

"No, indeed, it is quite so." His mother laughed, the smile returning to her lips. "I confess I was late to bed myself, although I did notice a young lady walking the hall-way." Even though she had not been invited, Lady Meyrick came to sit by the fire, her hands settling in her lap. "Miss Moir, I think."

The sound of her name jolted through Edward's frame, though he feigned indifference by a shrug.

"As I have said, I am sure many of the guests were late to bed last evening." He turned his eyes to the greenery above the fireplace rather than looking at his mother.

A small sigh broke, her shoulders dropping. "I did think Lord Ossington was particularly foolish last evening. The poor young lady must have been absolutely mortified."

Edward recalled how Miss Moir had practically run from the room, her cheeks scarlet as she had made her escape. His gut twisted. "Yes, Mother, she was." Edward let out a slow breath and, for the first time, his anger against Miss Moir began to fade a little. "I do not think Lord Ossington meant it in any other way other than jest, even if he was a little thoughtless in his going about it. Miss Moir informed me she has already forgiven him for it."

His mother laughed wryly. "I believe it was a little more than thoughtless, my dear son." Lady Meyrick shook her head, her laughter sharpening into a disappointed smile. "It was foolishness and nothing more. I confess I am surprised to hear she was so willing to forgive him so quickly. I assume he offered an apology to her?"

Edward opened his mouth to say, yes, his friend had, of course, apologized, only to realize the gentleman could not have done such a thing. He had not gone after Miss Moir, had not even seemed to realize his foolishness. In fact, had he not laughed as Miss Moir had quit the room? He had not even appeared to notice her absence nor link it to his foolishness. Certainly, Lord Ossington had *not* apologized... and yet Miss Moir had not held it against the gentleman.

"I do hope I have not upset you by remarking upon this." His mother drew in a long breath. "And I am sure you will be irritated with me in bringing up Miss Williams again, even though we are not speaking of her at present."

Edward groaned and immediately held up a hand, palm out. "Please, Mother, do not. I have enough to consider at the present moment, *and* it is Christmas Day also."

Lady Meyrick nodded slowly. "I am well aware it is Christmas Day," she said softly. "In speaking of the house party and all that has gone on within it, I thought only to explain to you why I have been pressing Miss Williams so dearly to your heart."

At this, Edward found himself sitting up a little straighter. "I should like to hear your reasons, certainly." His head tipped. "Although why you wish to tell me now when you have not done so beforehand, I cannot quite understand."

Lady Meyrick looked away, another sigh eliciting from her lips. "It was because I was afraid."

"Afraid?"

"Afraid you would turn from her, should you know the truth. If there had been even a hint of interest on your part, then I did not want to jeopardize it by revealing what I knew."

Something began to scurry through Edward's veins.

"And what is it you know?" His frown grew as his mother shifted in her chair and shook her head, saying nothing. To her eyes, she did appear to be a little distressed and his mother was not often in such a frame.

"My dear son." Lady Meyrick looked towards him. "You are a gentleman who is generous of heart."

This first remark had Edward wincing. "In that regard, Mother, I can assure you I have a great many failings." Recalling Miss Moir's sharp words to him, aware now of how much he had failed, his shoulders dropped. "I strive to be better, however."

His mother smiled softly. "Allow me to state, then, I have always found you generous of heart and of spirit. I will admit to you I took advantage of that spirit in organizing this house party without you being aware of it. I chose to inform you once it had all been planned, knowing you would agree."

Edward's forehead flickered. "You state, then, you arranged this house party with hidden motivations? It was not just meant to bring some cheer to the wintertime."

"I suppose my determinations were twofold." Lady Meyrick spread her hands. "Certainly I *did* want a little respite from the winter's difficulties." She shook her head. "But at the same time, it was not arranged for this reason alone."

Becoming a little irritated at his mother's lack of clarity, Edward rose from his chair, beginning to pace up and down the room as he waited for her to continue.

"I am aware I did you wrong in being less than truthful with you about this," Lady Meyrick sighed, now no longer looking at him but gazing at the fire. "However, I did it for my own reasons, which I do believe were good ones."

Edward threw up his hands. "What were those reasons? And what are they to do with Miss Williams?"

Lady Meyrick finally turned her face towards him. It was set into a somewhat sorrowful expression, and Edward's irritation quickly died away. Lady Meyrick's eyes were little glassy, her face pale and her hands clasped tightly together in her lap.

"Lord Jefferson has lost his fortune."

The words hung between them as Edward stopped pacing, his breath hitching as he turned to gaze directly into his mother's face. "He has lost his fortune?" His eyes closed tightly for a moment. "I do not understand."

"What is there to understand?" Lady Meyrick replied, shaking her head. "Lord Jefferson has made a fool of himself and lost all sense of responsibility when it comes to his wife and his daughter. He has been utterly reckless in his endeavors, has given way to gambling and thus no longer has a dowry for his daughter, nor enough financial support to continue living in his estate."

Edward winced, his shoulders dropping as a long breath escaped from him. It was not the first gentleman who would have made an unwise endeavor or two, but to lose himself in gambling was nothing but idiocy. His eyes closed, and he pinched the bridge of his nose as his mother murmured something more.

"Lady Jefferson is my friend. I had to do what I could for her."

"And you thought I would marry her daughter." Edward opened his eyes and saw his mother nod, the quivering smile on her lips speaking of great distress. On instinct, he walked to her and settled his hand on her shoulder, bending down to her. His mother grasped his hand quickly, tears beginning to spill from her eyes.

"I was afraid, if I told you the truth, you would push Miss Williams away." she explained, her shoulders now shaking a little. "Lady Jefferson is quite at a loss as to what she is to do. She is heartbroken over her husband's lack of consideration and devastated about what her daughter's future now may be. Given that Miss Williams is a pleasant, kind young lady, she might catch your eye... or at the very least, you might consider her if I were to encourage you. Engagement to Miss Williams would be the answer to one problem at the very least."

Blowing out his breath, Edward shook his head. "It is not our responsibility to fix such a situation."

Lady Meyrick nodded, but still held his gaze. "Be that as it may, my dear, we should always do whatever we can to help those we care for, should we not?" Letting go of his hand, she let out another heavy sigh. "She has tried so hard to correct her husband where he has erred, but he has not listened to her. Over the years, I have seen how he has crumbled her trust in him and become a gentleman so filled with disrepute, he cannot hold his head up within society." A faint tremor and the clenching of her hands betrayed her anger, although outwardly her expression remained without a trace of fury. "I wanted to do whatever I could so that my friend and her daughter did not face the bleakest of futures." Her eyes closed, another tear running down her cheek. "I went about it the wrong way. I understand that." She shook her head, pulling out her handkerchief and dabbing at her eyes as Edward crouched down so he might look up at his mother's face. "I do hope you can forgive me."

"There is nothing to forgive." Edward reached out and held her hand tightly. "You were doing so in an attempt to help a friend, to make a desperate situation better." Seeing how his mother nodded, Edward searched her face for a moment. "Does Lady Jefferson and Miss Williams have anywhere to live? If the estate must be given up, then –"

"I believe they will be as poor as church mice." Lady Meyrick swallowed hard, tears yet again threatening to fall as Edward squeezed her hand.

He licked his lips.

"Then you are to tell them to come and reside here."

His mother's eyes flew to his, staring at him, and Edward merely smiled.

"I could have twenty other families residing here, and should never even notice them," he remarked softly. "You can offer this to Lady Jefferson, although I wish to make clear my invitation is to Lady Jefferson and Miss Williams *only*." His smile faded. "Perhaps being apart from them will be what Lord Jefferson needs to realize the depths to which he has fallen." Squeezing her hand, he slowly got to his feet. "But pray understand, there shall be nothing between myself and Miss Williams. It is a kind thought and had circumstances been different, I might have considered her, but –"

"You cannot consider anyone else when you are already thinking of one particular lady," his mother interrupted, managing a smile as she wiped her eyes again. "You may pretend you have nothing of feeling for Miss Moir, but I am all too aware of it. She is an excellent young lady and I congratulate you on your choice. I do hope you will find success there."

Edward grimaced, thinking about all that had just taken place between himself and Miss Moir. "I am not certain there will be anything of note, Mother."

His mother made to open her mouth- no doubt to ask why – only for a very sharp knock to come to the door. Before Edward could even call for it to open, Lord

Ossington pushed it open and strode straight into the room, waving his hands about.

"I do beg your pardon, Your Grace, but I could not wait."

Lady Meyrick coughed softly and Lord Ossington glanced to her, clearly having only just seen her, given the way his eyes flared.

"Again. I can only apologize," Lord Ossington started to say, only to think better of it. Stopping, he ran one hand through his hair. "I was spoken to this morning by Lady Sutton."

Edward cleared his throat, noting his mother's meaningful glance. "You spoke to Lady Sutton," he repeated as the gentleman nodded. "Or rather, she came to speak with you."

Lord Ossington wrung his hands. "You cannot know how sorrowful I am," he continued, shaking his head to himself. "I truly was the most foolish of gentlemen. I should never have done such a thing, especially after you asked me to keep your previous conversation with the lady quite secret."

Edward wanted to drop his head into his hands, aware of how his mother's eyebrows had lifted, but instead he kept his face as expressionless as he could, looking straight back at Lord Ossington.

"I did you a great wrong," Lord Ossington continued. "I am sure I embarrassed you a great deal."

"It is not me who you humiliated!" Edward's exclamation rang around the room. "You embarrassed Miss Moir much more than I. Can you not understand that? Why is it you are coming to speak with me rather than going to her?"

Lord Ossington shrugged, dropping his hands. "Because I cannot find the lady," he told Edward plainly. "Her mother states Miss Moir may stay in her room for a good part of the day. If that is my doing, then I am truly sorry and I did beg the lady to convey my apologies. I thought then to come to you also and express just how sorry I am for my thoughtlessness."

Immediately, every instinct within Edward urged him towards Miss Moir, pushing him to hurry up to her room, to rap on the door and inquire as to whether or not she was unwell – and if he was the cause of it. Taking a breath, he closed his eyes and let it out again slowly, reminding himself he could not let any depth of feeling sweep him away into foolish actions. Was he not still angry with her? Was he not frustrated over all she had done? Why then was he suddenly so eager to go back to her side once more?

"I do apologize again, Your Grace."

Edward waved one hand in his direction, eager to dismiss his friend. "Very well, Lord Ossington, your apology is accepted. As regards Miss Moir, please do leave the lady in peace. You may not be the cause of her distress." Taking a breath and ignoring the sharp look from his mother, Edward spread both hands. "Please do not concern yourself any longer."

"But of course." Still muttering apologies, Lord Ossington removed himself from their company, walking backwards until he was able to close the door and leave both Edward and Lady Meyrick alone once more.

"It seems all is not well between yourself and Miss Moir." His mother lifted an eyebrow. "Is it something you have done?"

Edward flung out one hand, turning sharply away from his mother's penetrating gaze. "It is something we have *both* done."

"And have you spoken to her of this matter?"

"Of course I have." His response was little gruffer than he had intended, but his mother did not appear to take it badly, for she merely smiled back at Edward – much to his infuriation when he glanced at her.

"Then I am sure things between you can easily be resolved."

Edward shook his head. "I am not so sure."

"Nonsense." Lady Meyrick tossed her head. "All such matters can be settled, particularly when it is Christmas. I am sure there is nothing the two if you cannot sort out if, indeed, you have an affection for each other.... an affection you want to continue with, I presume." A meaningful look was sent in Edward's direction, and he let out a heavy sigh, resisting the urge to roll his eyes at the way his mother was persisting.

"Yes, Mother, it is an affection I wish to continue." Admitting it was, in fact, something of a relief, only to be followed by a sinking sense of dread as he remembered how he had practically banished Miss Moir from his presence the previous evening. Now the shock had worn off and now he had opportunity to think about what had happened, he found himself no longer as frustrated nor as upset. In fact, he slowly began to understand her actions. They had not been right, certainly, but there had been reason – maybe even a good reason – behind what she had done.

"Besides which, you are a forgiving sort." His mother smiled at him and got out of her chair. "I do not think you will have any difficulty in forgiving Miss Moir for whatever she has done to upset you. And no doubt, since she is so very kind of spirit, she will have forgiven you already, just as she did with Lord Ossington."

More than a little surprised to hear his mother speaking

so highly of him, Edward blinked rapidly. "And what would make you say so?"

His mother gestured towards the door, tilting her head a little to the left, her eyes bright. "Look how quickly you forgave Lord Ossington for his foolishness last evening."

Upon hearing her words, Edward's heart sank. It was not as though his mother was speaking untruths, for yes, he had accepted the apology very quickly indeed and had been glad to give his forgiveness. So why had he not done so with Miss Moir?

"And consider your reaction to my revelations also," his mother added gently. "I have spoken to you of the wrong I have done in deceiving you, in keeping from you the truth about Miss Williams and her family. Yet again, you listened, you considered, you understood, and you forgave. *That* is why I say you are a forgiving sort, because you have proven that to me."

Edward's heart dropped to all the lower, to the point he was not certain it would ever return to him. His heaviness must have shown in his expression, for his mother drew back towards him and settled one hand on his arm.

"Whatever is the matter?"

"I have not behaved so with Miss Moir." Admitting it aloud was difficult enough, but seeing his mother's surprised expression was all the more shaming.

"She came to me with her wrongdoing, having attempted to speak to me of it twice already. I did not give her opportunity to finish those conversations, however, and now when she finally found the chance to do, I became very angry with her. She gave me her reasons, much as you have done, and her reasons were not for herself, but rather for the good of others... just as yours were."

Lady Meyrick blinked. Her head lifted, and she stepped

back as she looked up into his face, but Edward could not meet her gaze.

"I am surprised to hear you have held something against Miss Moir." The softness of her tone made Edward want to groan aloud over his foolishness. "Is there a reason that you have done such a thing?"

Edward licked his lips. As yet, he could not give an explanation for it. Was it because he had held her in higher regard than he ought? Or had he simply been so astonished he had allowed his anger to be the pervading feeling?

"I did not give myself opportunity to think." Correcting himself, he shook his head. "I *chose* not to give myself opportunity to think about it all before responding. I behaved poorly, Mother. She was so very desperate to tell me the truth, despite knowing there might be consequences in doing so. In fact," he continued, a sudden awareness creeping over him, "she could very easily have hidden her guilt from me."

Had Miss Moir decided, Edward realized, she could have found out which figurine she had taken, merely by asking one of the staff or bringing it into conversation. Thereafter, she could have returned it by one way or the other and thus would have absolved herself entirely of any responsibility. No one would have known of it, and no doubt, he would have thought the pawnbroker had been mistaken about the item. He would have perhaps considered the figurine being absent was only due to a maid's carelessness. Miss Moir could have kept everything back from him, but instead, she had told him the truth.... and he had rejected her because of it.

"Is that not the mark of a very humble character?" His mother's smile softened as Edward looked back at her. "To be willing to be open about one's fault, of one's mistakes and to be honest about where we have failed. It speaks of a meekness, of a gentleness of character and considerate heart. She may have wronged you in some way but I would not hold it against her. We all do wrong at times, do we not?"

Edward rubbed one hand over his eyes, his breath heavy. "She did not hold my wrongs against me." Murmuring to himself, he did not see how his mother's eyebrows lifted. It was only when she turned away that he finally looked at her again.

"I shall go see to the guests." Lady Meyrick smiled back at him, making for the door. "You require time to resolve things with the lady. I understand. I will keep them as contented as can be until our Christmas dinner."

Edward shook his head. "I do not know what I can do. If she is keeping to her room, then what right have I to demand her company?"

With her hand on the door, his mother looked back at him steadily. "She will come if you ask her."

No flicker of hope flared in Edward's heart. "How can you be so certain?"

"Because love is not as fleeting as you think," came the soft reply. "This is the time of year where we consider the love which has been offered to us, where we think of hope, of forgiveness of wrongdoing. Carry that with you when you speak with her. Tell her of your heart. I am certain all will be well."

As the door closed, Edward sighed heavily and dropped into a chair. Lowering his head, he thrust his hands into his hair, his elbows on his knees and his back rounding. He had not been considerate. He had not thought of anything, save for his anger and frustration and surprise over what she had done. How much more considered he might have been in this situation, had he given himself opportunity just to take a few moments to think! He might then have had a chance to speak to Miss Moir about what he wanted from their acquaintance, instead of pushing her so very far away. Yet, however, a tiny flare began to lift through his heart. Perhaps his mother was right. Perhaps this *was* the season for forgiveness, for new things and for the love that could forgive wrongdoing. He had not displayed such a love to Miss Moir, but if she gave him another opportunity, then he would prove it to her again.

The only question was whether she would be willing to speak with him.

CHAPTER TWELVE

Glancing at her reflection, Augusta took in the shadows under her eyes. She had slept poorly, tossing and turning, her dreams filled with an angry Duke throwing her not only from his library but also from his house. One arm outstretched, one finger pointing and her sobbing into her mother's shoulder as the carriage drove them back home. It had been a dreadful dream and one she prayed would have no truth to it.

On this Christmas Day, she did not know where she stood with the Duke of Meyrick. His anger had been obvious, but Augusta accepted it, believing she deserved it. She had stolen from him. Yes, she had tried to make amends, had tried to bring it back, but it had not taken away her guilt. Part of her wished she had never chosen to be truthful with the Duke, that she had simply found a way to put the figurine back without ever telling him about it.... but her heart would not have allowed her to do it. It would have weighed down so heavily, she would have struggled to even draw a breath in his company. She would not have been able to smile or laugh, would not have been able to accept any furthering of their connection, not until she had told him the truth. In that regard, she was glad she had done so, for there was nothing weighing on her conscience any longer, but the consequences of what she had done were a heavy burden to shoulder. Her mother had come in earlier to ask her if she intended to break her fast, but by then Augusta had already ordered a tray. She had dined quietly in her room, then risen to stand and look out over the falling snow.... and felt her heart so painful, it had been a fight to draw breath.

Is this what it feels like when love is taken away?

Tears filled her eyes, her reflection suddenly morose, and she twisted her head away, not wanting to see the grief in the mirror. This Christmas Day had meant to be a joyous time, when she had been filled with happiness, with a bright and beautiful hope for the future, and instead there was nothing but dreariness and darkness. The Duke would not turn her from his house as she had dreamt, but it did not mean he would not turn her from his heart. She would never have another opportunity to draw near to him, sure now her heart would cling to him forever. Regardless of whether anything came to be between them, she would always hold him there. Perhaps it was to be her punishment: her heart continually aching over the gentleman she loved, and what could have been had she not behaved with such idiocy. It would be her warning never to do so again.

A slight scratch came to the door and Augusta called for the servant to enter. The maid stepped in, bobbed a curtsy and handed her a note before hurrying away. A little surprised, Augusta turned it over, opening it quickly... only for her heart to shoot towards the ceiling.

The Duke of Meyrick wanted to speak with her.

Instantly scolding herself for her foolishness, Augusta

drew in another breath. The Duke might want to speak to her but it did not mean he would want to repair what was broken, might not seek out any sort of reparation. Instead, he might wish to sever their connection completely instead; this could be his judgment, their time of ending. It did not mean she had any hope whatsoever. Mayhap she ought to expect the worst, given just how poorly she had behaved.

Glancing back at her reflection, Augusta took in a breath, pushed back her shoulders and lifted her chin. She did not look as though she had been crying, at least although her heart was still very much in a state of sorrow. There was a weight upon it, a weight she feared would never leave her, regardless of the outcome with the Duke of Meyrick. There was no question over as to whether she would go to speak with him or not, for what a Duke asked for, a Duke received – although she had not offered him that dance back in the summer Season! It might have been the only time he had ever been refused something!

A rueful smile pulled at her mouth as she rose to her feet, pinching her cheeks lightly so as to add a little color. In this case, however, what the Duke requested from her she was more than willing to give, even if it did mean the ending of all her hopes. Nervousness tumbled through her stomach as she made her way from the room and directly towards the Duke's study, where the gentleman in question would be waiting for her.

The study door was ajar as she approached it and Augusta took a moment to steady herself before she rapped on the door, her eyes closing. Something within her begged her to turn around, to hurry from the Duke's study and back to the safety of her room so his conversation could be pushed to the side– but before she could listen to it, Augusta forced her hand to reach to knock at the door. The sound rang around the hallway and she sucked in a breath, aware of the nervous anxiety which spread into every part of her frame.

A rush of air had her opening her eyes. The Duke stood there, looming forward in the doorway, one hand on the door frame, the other reaching out towards her as if he wanted to take her hand.

"Miss Moir." His eyes closed for just a moment as he dropped his hand. "Thank you so much for coming. I did not think you would be willing to attend me after our discussion last evening." Stepping aside, he gestured to the empty room. "Might you be willing to step inside? I can send for a maid or leave the door wide open."

"I am sure the latter would be quite suitable." Still entirely uncertain as to what it was he wished to discuss with her, Augusta let her worry settle into the pit of her stomach as she took in deep breaths. Her feet were heavier than they had ever been, her legs struggling to put one in front of the other as she walked slowly into the Duke's study. Aware of his presence close behind her, a shiver ran down her frame. She did not know where to stand, looking around the room and immediately finding her eyes were drawn to the table in the corner where she had taken the figurine in the first place. Her cheeks seared as she dragged her eyes away, dropping her head and standing with her hands clasped in the middle of the room.

"Please, do come and sit by the fire." The Duke moved past her and Augusta followed, relieved she would be able to sit for fear her legs would not hold her up much longer such was the state of her nervousness. "I do not want you to be at all ill at ease," the Duke continued as Augusta settled herself in an overstuffed chair, relieved the warmth of the fire was near to her. Her hands were already rather cold –

although it was not from the chill, given that the room was very warm indeed.

"You do not mind if I sit opposite you, do you?"

Augusta shook her head wordlessly. The Duke of Meyrick could sit wherever he wished, given that this was his study and she was only a guest, but she could not give voice to such thoughts. In fact, she could not seem to voice anything for her throat was dry and nothing came to mind.

"First of all, I should like you to know Lord Ossington came to speak with me."

Augusta's eyes flared. Were they only to speak of Lord Ossington and of what he had done the previous evening? Was this the only reason the Duke wanted her here?

"I believe your mother spoke to him and made it quite clear how much he had embarrassed you - embarrassed us both, in fact. His apology was meant to come direct to you, but he was not able to reach you."

Dropping her gaze to her clasped hands, Augusta took a moment before she replied. "I have been in my room this morning." She did not give any further explanation than that, nor any reason for it, for surely, the Duke would be able to deduce why she had done such a thing!

"Of course." Clearing his throat, the Duke took another few moments before he continued. The silence was unbearable, and many times, Augusta herself tried to speak, but nothing came. She was frustrated with herself with her lack of ability to even make the smallest conversation but after last evening, it was as though she did not know how to respond to him. It was as if he were an entirely different gentleman - one she would have to get to know all over again. – if she was given the chance.

Continuing to sit, Augusta hastily glanced towards the Duke, struggling to hold the anxiety within her as it tumbled freely, spreading fresh frissons of nervous energy to the tips of her fingers and toes. She clenched her hands tightly in an attempt to get rid of some of the strain which bound her. Why was he saying nothing? Why was he simply looking at her?

"Do you have anything you wish to say about Lord Ossington?"

Augusta blinked. Yet again, he was speaking of Lord Ossington. Perhaps this was all he wanted to say to her. Perhaps there was nothing else for them to discuss. It seemed almost inevitable now she was to be entirely frustrated, and the end of their acquaintance was immediately on the horizon.

"It is good Lord Ossington intends to apologize." Even to her own ears, her voice was nothing but a quaver. "I am grateful for it, at least, though within my heart, I bear him no grudge."

The Duke looked away. His hands now clasped together as hers were, his elbows on his knees as he dropped his head for a moment.

"I - I am sure he will apologize to you personally also, should you wish it." Was this what the Duke was concerned about? "It is clear the gentleman sees he has behaved foolishly."

The Duke lifted his head. "You are not angry with him?"

Augusta hesitated, catching the flicker in the Duke of Meyrick's eyes. Was he continuing to talk about Lord Ossington with such a question, or was there something more there?

"Lord Ossington behaved as he did, simply because he thought it mirthful. I do not think he gave much consideration to anything else. He wanted only to join in with the parlor game. And therefore I do not feel as though I can hold much against him."

The Duke closed his eyes tight for a moment before lowering his head a little more. "You are a good deal more forgiving than I, Miss Moir." His eyes caught hers for the briefest moment. "For you, forgiveness comes quickly. Mine, it seems, does not." Grimacing as he spoke, the Duke shook his head and Augusta opened her mouth to ask him what he meant, only for him to continue. "My mother was with me earlier. She congratulated me on having a forgiving spirit, stating it was something she had seen within me. For I quickly forgave Lord Ossington for his mistake and, in turn, also my mother when she apologized for her part in keeping something from me." A heavy sigh broke from him, and sitting up, he spread his hands. "Which then brings me to the question as to why I am so determined to hold things against *you*, Miss Moir."

Augusta's heart turned over. Finally, he held her gaze, no longer pulling his eyes away. There was a heaviness set into his expression that pushed his eyebrows down. His jaw was tight, his lips thin, and his green eyes had never appeared so dull. Had she done something else to injure him? Was he about to tell her, regardless of her reasons for taking the figurine, he did not think his forgiveness would come to her in the same way?

"Again, Miss Moir, it appears as though I acted rashly. I allowed the shock to overwhelm me, the surprise at hearing what you had done was utterly astonishing."

Something like a gasp of relief left her, glad he had not told her all was ended. "I can understand why it would come as such a surprise," she managed to say, fighting to look at him, a fresh hope setting a light to the smoldering candle deep within her soul. "I swear to you, such behavior is not something I often indulge in."

A wry smile was sent back to her. "In that regard, I do not often have cause to be so angry, and in truth, I have little practice in pulling back my temper."

"But you had cause to be angry."

Without warning, the Duke rose to his feet and Augusta's breath swirled about her chest, her heart clanging.

"I was a brute." The Duke began to march around the room, his arms flailing all the while. "I treated those widows with carelessness, taking out my frustrations upon them for no good reason. There was no need for me to be so ill-considered. I have learned, Miss Moir, that had I simply spoken to my mother, had I been calm and quiet, I might have found out the truth as to why she did such things. What my mother did was not right, but it was understandable. She had good intentions... just as you had."

Augusta's gaze was fixed and steady as the Duke spoke, his words almost impossible to grasp a hold of. The way he was speaking was so utterly astonishing, she could barely comprehend what he was saying. Was he truly offering her his apology? Did he mean every word he said?

Before she could respond, the Duke swung around to face her, his hands now by his sides. "Miss Moir, allow me to speak plainly. My mother has pushed me towards a particular young lady. I will not go into the circumstances, but needless to say, her reasons for doing so was an attempt to aid the young lady and her mother."

Still burning with surprise, Augusta opened her mouth, but no sound came out.

"And you, Miss Moir," the Duke continued, taking a small step towards her. "You took a figurine from my table because I was not generous in the way I ought to have been. Indeed, you gave up your own coin also, did you not?"

Nodding, Augusta swallowed hard, trying to say she did not expect the Duke of Meyrick to forgive her, only for him to smile back at her mumbling.

"You may have been wrong to do such a thing, but you did it to aid another." The Duke of Merrick shook his head, passing one hand over his forehead. "When I noticed one of my trinkets was absent, I did not feel any overwhelming concern. I have many ornaments, many trinkets, many coins, Miss Moir. I say these things not to boast to you but rather to express how much generosity I should have in return."

The tightness in her throat remained, but Augusta managed to squeeze out her words regardless. "You speak very honestly, Your Grace."

"Which is just as I ought." The Duke flung out both hands either side. "I come, Miss Moir, to tell you of my faults and my failings, which I fear you are becoming all too aware of. I ought not to have pushed you from my sight. I ought not to have given you the impression that my anger was too great to be overcome. From this day onwards, I shall seek to do everything well, Miss Moir, if only you would give me the chance to do so."

The logs in the fireplace crackled furiously as Augusta stared at the Duke of Meyrick, seeing the flicker in his eyes, watching his hands fall back to his sides. Had she heard him correctly? Had he truly asked her such a thing?

"Miss Moir?" The Duke of Merrick stood tall, one hand lifting it out towards her, which, as the silence grew and her gaze became fixed, slowly fell back towards his side. The flash in his eyes began to fade; the heaviness began to settle into his expression again.

"You take your guilt so heavily upon yourself, Your Grace." Finally managing to speak, Augusta continued to stare up at him, not certain her legs would bear her weight should she stand. "Have we both not made mistakes? Should we both not forgive one another? I do not hold you responsible. I, instead, look at my own foolish actions and regret them deeply. If you are willing to overlook my faults, if you are truly willing to forgive what I have done, then how could I not offer the very same forgiveness in return?"

The Duke's jaw worked as he closed his eyes for a long moment. The room was near silence, heavy with tension. Then, at the very next second, the Duke strode across the room, caught her hands, and pulled her close to him.

Augusta accepted his embrace with both relief and joy, having been afraid his nearness was something she would never experience again. And yet now, here she was, wrapped in his arms. She had dreamed of this but had never imagined his returning closeness would be so incredibly powerful. Her heart wanted to throw itself towards the skies. Her eyes began to brim with tears as she rested her head on his shoulder, stifling a sob.

"I am sorry for the pain you have endured, my love." The Duke's voice murmured softly in her ear as Augusta battled with her emotions, attempting to compose herself but quite unable to do so. "I am sorry for the trouble and the trial you had been forced to endure for my sake. I am not a man who is without fault, Miss Moir, but I am a gentleman who is willing to admit such faults and who, instead, seeks to improve day by day. When I am with you, Miss Moir, the only thing I want is to be the very best of gentlemen and I am certain, with you by my side, I will be able to do that."

Finally strong enough to lift her head from his shoulder, Augusta leaned back a little so she might look into his eyes.

They were vivid and alive with all she yearned for, and she found herself smiling.

"You must know how deeply I am in love with you." The willingness to speak threw her words from her lips. "When I carried my burden of guilt upon my shoulders, I knew I could not tell you the truth of my heart. Now, with it gone, I am able to make my declaration to you, glad my heart can be free enough to tell you of the affection it holds."

The Duke of Meyrick's hand lifted from her waist to brush down her cheek. "Again, you astonish me, Miss Moir. How you can hold an affection for me after everything I have forced you to endure is beyond my comprehension."

"I am not without fault, Your Grace." Augusta smiled back at him, her vision still a little blurred by tears. "But I am glad to be able to speak of my affection for you now. Try as I might, I could not rid myself of it and thus it has only lingered and grown to such proportions, I can call it nothing but love."

A gentle, curious smile touched the Duke's mouth. "I should be very obliged to you if you would let me kiss you, Miss Moir."

Augusta smiled back at him, a curl of excitement rippling through her. "If you are to do so, Your Grace, I think it would be perfectly appropriate for you to call me Augusta."

The Duke chuckled softly, the sound running lately over Augusta's skin as she shivered in expectant delight. When he lowered his head, her eyes closed involuntarily of their own accord and when his lips touched hers, it was as though the world had turned itself upside down before righting itself again. The sensation was encapsulating, pulling away her breath, stealing her heart all over again.

She sighed against his mouth and leaned into him all the more, her hands at his shoulders, his arm around her waist. The Duke ended their kiss far too soon for Augusta's liking, but he merely smiled down at her, his hand at her cheek again.

"I dare not linger, Miss Moir, for fear we will be seen. I do not wish to do anything which would cause you more difficulty."

Augusta found herself laughing softly as the Duke's eyebrows lifted in question. "To be caught with you, Your Grace, I would not consider any difficulty whatsoever."

The Duke of Meyrick laughed but took a step back, making sure to keep their hands joined. "If it is truly how you feel, Miss Moir, then there is something more I should like to ask you."

Augusta looked up at him with a soft smile. With the fire crackling beside them, greenery adorning the room and the snow falling gently outside, she was quite sure whatever the Duke asked of her, she would oblige him.

"You have spoken of your heart, so filled with an affection, it will never be gone from you," the Duke began, his smile no longer present, but the seriousness steadying his gaze. "My heart is the same, Augusta. I confess I love you. I want nothing more than this love to grow all the deeper and thus, my desire now is to offer you my hand... that is, if you will have me."

Augusta's eyes flared wide, her heart coming to a stop as she stared into the Duke's handsome face and realized what he was offering her. To be in love with the Duke, to have him embrace her, their hearts as one, was one thing, but to be asked to be his bride was quite another. She had never expected it, had not allowed himself to believe there was any hope of it – and yet, his question remained. Something like a squeak came by way of her answer and the Duke suddenly grinned, sending heat searing into Augusta's face. She dropped her head only for gentle fingers to lift her chin so that once more she was looking into his eyes.

"Last evening, when all of the gifts were given me, the only thing I was thinking about was you." The quietness of his voice spoke of the tenderness he held in his heart. "As ridiculous as Lord Ossington was, he did bring me the very best gift. *You* are a gift to me, Augusta. Your sweetness, your kindness, your forthright manner, and your determination to do what is right are things I do not think I can be without. I want to marry you, Augusta. Tell me if you will be my bride."

With a boldness which surprised even herself, Augusta pushed herself up and kissed him again, her hands twining around his neck.

"I love you," she murmured gently against his mouth. "To be asked such a thing is an honor indeed. How can I not accept? All I wish for in this life is to share my days with you."

The Duke dropped his head and kissed her lightly again, his hand again by her cheek. "You are the most precious of all gifts," he told her softly as she gazed up into the eyes of the man she loved. "My Christmas Day has never been happier."

"We shall be together, our hearts as one, our love holding us fast throughout this Christmas," she whispered, smiling. "Not for only this Christmas, but all the Christmases to come."

He kissed her again. "And all the days in between."

.   .   .

She didn't want to marry a Duke, yet love overcame her objections! Love it!

If you missed the first book in the Christmas Kisses series, get caught up right now! The Lady's Christmas Kiss Read ahead a few pages for a sneak peek! Read this one? Try another Christmas favorite of mine A Family for Christmas

The Returned Lords of Grosvenor Square
The Returned Lords of Grosvenor Square: A Regency
Romance Boxset
The Waiting Bride
The Long Return
The Duke's Saving Grace
A New Home for the Duke

The Spinsters Guild
The Spinsters Guild: A Sweet Regency Romance Boxset
A New Beginning
The Disgraced Bride
A Gentleman's Revenge
A Foolish Wager
A Lord Undone

Convenient Arrangements
Convenient Arrangements: A Regency Romance
Collection
A Broken Betrothal
In Search of Love
Wed in Disgrace
Betrayal and Lies
A Past to Forget
Engaged to a Friend

Landon House
Landon House: A Regency Romance Boxset
Mistaken for a Rake
A Selfish Heart
A Love Unbroken
A Christmas Match
A Most Suitable Bride

An Expectation of Love

Second Chance Regency Romance
Second Chance Regency Romance Boxset
Loving the Scarred Soldier
Second Chance for Love
A Family of her Own
A Spinster No More

Soldiers and Sweethearts
Soldiers and Sweethearts: A Sweet Regency Romance
Boxset
To Trust a Viscount
Whispers of the Heart
Dare to Love a Marquess
Healing the Earl
A Lady's Brave Heart

Ladies on their Own: Governesses and Companions
More Than a Companion
The Hidden Governess
The Companion and the Earl
More than a Governess
Protected by the Companion
A Wager with a Viscount

Lost Fortunes, Found Love
A Viscount's Stolen Fortune
For Richer, For Poorer
Her Heart's Choice

Christmas Stories

Christmas Kisses (Series)
The Lady's Christmas Kiss
A Viscount's Christmas Queen
Her Christmas Duke

Love and Christmas Wishes: Three Regency Romance
Novellas
A Family for Christmas
Mistletoe Magic: A Regency Romance
Heart, Homes & Holidays: A Sweet Romance Anthology

Happy Reading!

All my love,

Rose

A SNEAK PEEK OF A LADY'S CHRISTMAS KISS

PROLOGUE

"I have wonderful news!"

Rebecca looked up at her mother, but then immediately turned her head away. Lady Wilbram often came with news and, much of the time, it was nothing more than idle gossip; something that Rebecca herself did not enjoy listening to.

"Yes, Mama?" She did not so much as even look up from her embroidery, but rather continued to sew. The long, bleak winter stretched out before her, dreary and dismal – much like the state of her heart at present – and with very little to cheer her. Her father, the Earl of Wilbram, had made it clear that he was not to go to London for the little Season and thus, Rebecca was to be stuck at home, having only her mother for company. No doubt there would be a great deal more of this sort of occurrence, whereby her mother would burst into the room, expressing great delight at some news or other and, in doing so, remind Rebecca of just how far away she was from it all.

Although I am not certain that I wish to return to

London at present. There is the chance that he would be there and I do not think I could bear to see him.

"Rebecca. You are not as much as even listening to me!"

Out of the corner of her eye, Rebecca caught how her mother threw up her hands, but merely smiled quietly. "I am paying you a *great* deal of attention, Mother," she answered, silently thinking to herself that it was the only thing she *could* do, given just how determined her mother was. Having been quite contented with her own thoughts, it was a little frustrating to have been interrupted so.

"You shall soon drop your embroidery once you realize what it is I have to tell you." The promise in her mother's voice was one that finally caught Rebecca's interest, but telling herself not to be foolish, she threw only a quick smile in her mother's direction.

"Yes, I am sure I shall," she promised softly. "Please, tell me what it is. I am almost beside myself with anticipation." Her sarcasm obviously laid heavy on her mother's shoulders, for she immediately threw up her hands in clear disgust.

"Well, if you must behave so, then I shall not tell you the contents of this letter. You shall not know of it! And *I* shall be the one to go to the Duke's Christmas... affair."

Rebecca blinked, her gaze still fixed down upon her embroidery, but her hand stilling on the needle. Had she heard her mother correctly? Had she, in fact, said the words Duke and Christmas? Her stomach tightened perceptively, and she looked up, her irritation suddenly forgotten.

"*Now* I have your attention."

Her mother's eyebrows lifted and Rebecca set her embroidery down completely, her hands going to her lap. "Yes, Mama, now you have my attention," This was said rather quickly and with a slight flippancy, which Rebecca was certain her mother would hear in her voice, but she did not seem to respond. Seeing her mother's shoulders drop after a moment, her hands going to her sides again, Rebecca let out a slow breath. Evidently, she was forgiven already.

"Yes, I did say the Duke – the Duke of Meyrick, in fact – and I *did* say Christmas."

"What is it he has invited us to?"

"A Christmas house party. It is a little unusual, for it appears to be longer than many others would be. But then again, I suppose as the Duke of Meyrick, he is quite able to do as he pleases!"

"How wonderful!" In an instant, the grey winter seemed to fade from her eyes, no longer held out before her as the only path she had to take. Instead, she had an opportunity for happiness, enjoyment, laughter and smiles – as well as the fact that there would be very little chance of being in company with *him*. No doubt he was either back at his estate or would return to London for the little Season.

"We shall have to speak to your father, of course."

At this, Rebecca's heart plunged to the ground, splintering as it fell. Her father had only just declared that he would remain at his estate over the winter. Even if there *was* an invitation to a most prestigious house party, the chances of him agreeing to attend were very small indeed. Scowling up at her mother, she turned her head away. Why had she told her something such as this only for it to be snatched away again?

"Even if your father should not wish to attend, there is no reason you and I cannot both go," her mother continued immediately, turning Rebecca's scowl into a smile of delight. "He will understand – and given that his estate is not very far from our own, the journey will not be a difficult one. Besides which, it is an excellent occasion for you to make further acquaintances in preparation for the summer season... that is, unless you have any desire to find a gentleman suitor this Christmas."

Rebecca laughed, shaking her head at her mother's twinkling eyes and forcing herself not to think of *him*. Given that her mother and father knew nothing about the affair and, therefore, the abrupt ending to what had taken place, she did not think it wise to inform them of it. "Mama, I am very glad indeed we have been invited. I go with no expectation, just as you ought to do."

Lady Wilbram smiled warmly. "You are quite correct. Now we must make preparations to attend this house party. You will need to look through your gowns and decide which of them is the most suitable. We have time to purchase one or two new gowns also, for there is certain to be at least one Christmas ball! You must be prepared for every possible occasion." Making her way back towards the door with purposeful steps, as though she intended to begin such preparations immediately, Lady Wilbram threw a glance back at Rebecca. Understanding that she was meant to go after her mother, Rebecca set her embroidery down and followed immediately, her heart light and filled with hope.

"Prepared for every occasion, Mama?" she asked as her mother nodded firmly. "What exactly is it that I ought to expect from such a house party? I have only been to one before and it lasted only three days. There was very little that could be done by way of occasion."

"You will find the Duke's house parties are very different experiences," her mother told her, grasping her hand warmly as they walked through the door. "You must have every expectation and, at the same time, no expectation. That is why we must be prepared for every eventuality, making certain that you have an outfit suitable for whatever it is the Duke might decide to do. Christmas is such a wonderful season, is it not?"

Rebecca laughed softly at her mother's excited expression and the delight in her voice. "Made all the more wonderful by this house party," she agreed, wondering how she was going to contain her anticipation for the few weeks before the house party began. "I am looking forward to it. It seems as though winter will not be so mediocre after all."

After being introduced to everyone, Rebecca took her seat beside her very dear friend, Miss Augusta Moir, whom she was very glad to see. They had exchanged letters quite frequently, and when news of the house party reached Rebecca, one of the first things she did had been to write to Augusta. How glad she was to receive Augusta's letter back, and how delighted to know that she would also be present!

"And that is almost all of us!" Lady Meyrick put her hands out wide, welcoming them all. "There are only one or two other guests still to arrive. I do not know why they have been delayed, but that does not mean we cannot continue. We will soon begin our festivities and they will join us when they are able. Pray, enjoy your conversations for a few minutes longer and, thereafter, the first of our games will begin!"

Rebecca glanced around the room, looking at each and every face and recognizing only a few of them. She did not know exactly who else would arrive, but the company here seemed to be quite delightful. In addition to the fact that she had her dear friend Augusta present also, she was quite convinced it would be an excellent few weeks.

"I do wonder what such festivities will be," Speaking in a hushed whisper, Miss Moir leaned towards Rebecca. "I have heard the Duke is something of an extravagant fellow. Perhaps that will mean this holiday house party will be an exceptional one."

"Yes, but *all* Dukes are known to be extravagant fellows," Rebecca reminded her friend, chuckling. "I would expect nothing less. Although," she continued. "I do wonder where the Duke himself is."

"Did you not greet him when you arrived? He was waiting on the steps to make certain that we were greeted. I certainly was made to feel very welcome by his mother!"

"Yes, he did do so." Remembering the slightly pinched expression on the Duke's face when he had greeted both her and her mother, Rebecca allowed her own concern to remain. "He did not appear to be very glad to see us, however. I will say that for him."

Her friend nodded slowly, her gaze drifting around the room as murmurs of conversation continued between the other guests. "He did not smile once, and certainly I found him rather stiff. His mother, on the other hand, was quite the opposite."

"Mayhap he simply does not like the cold, and given the Season, it is rather cold."

Her friend nodded in agreement, although Rebecca did not miss the twinkle in her friend's eyes. "It is almost as though he does not realize it is wintertime," she remarked, making Rebecca laugh. Her laughter changed into a sigh. "Perhaps he is as I am, in waiting and hoping for the summer to return," Her mind grew suddenly heavy, and she looked away. "I confess I struggle with this long winter. My mood is much improved now that my father has permitted me to come to this house party, however."

Miss Moir laughed softly. "And I am also grateful for your presence here. I am, as you know, a little shy, and I confess that not knowing a great many people here as yet has allowed my anxiety to rise a little."

"You have no need to be at all anxious," Rebecca replied firmly. "You are more than handsome, come from an excellent family and you are well able to have many a conversation with both gentlemen and ladies." She lifted one eyebrow. "At times, I think you pretend this anxiety is a part of your character, for I do not think I would be aware of it otherwise."

"I swear to you, I do not pretend!" Miss Moir exclaimed, only to let out a chuckle and to shake her head, realizing that Rebecca was teasing her. "Do you hope to meet anyone of interest here? Or shall you only be interested in furthering your acquaintances? Christmas is a time where many a gentleman will seek to steal a kiss!"

Hesitating, Rebecca wondered how she was to answer. Her friend was entirely unaware of how her heart had been broken this last Season. Indeed, neither her mother nor her father was aware of it either, but she had borne this heavy weight for many months. The pain lingered still, and there was only one gentleman that she was to blame for it. Her mother and her friends might be hopeful that she would acquaint herself with a gentleman of note with the hope that perhaps the match would be made in the summer Season, but for the present, Rebecca was quite contented to have only acquaintances – and nothing more. Her heart was still too damaged. It certainly had not been healed enough for her to even *think* about becoming closely acquainted with another gentleman.

"Lady Rebecca?"

Rebecca blinked quickly, and then silently demanded that she smile in response. "Forgive me, I became a little lost in thought." Shrugging, she looked away. "I think I should be glad of new acquaintances for the present at least. I do not want nor require anything else."

"I quite understand," Miss Moir looked away, just as Rebecca turned her gaze back towards her friend. Rebecca chose to say nothing further, waiting until her friend looked back at her before she continued the conversation.

"What do you think shall be our first game?" With a quick breath, she returned their topic of conversation to the house party itself. She did not want to go into any particular details about what had happened the previous season, given that a good deal of it was still a secret.

Miss Moir clapped her hands lightly. "I do hope it will be something that will make us all laugh and smile so that there is no awkwardness between any of us any longer." Excitement shone in her eyes, and Rebecca could not help but smile.

"Perhaps there will be some Christmas games! Out of all the ones you can think of, which one would be your favorite?"

The two considered this for some minutes and, thereafter, fell into a deep discussion about whether the Twelfth Night cake or Snapdragon was the very best game. But eventually, their conversation was cut short by Lady Meyrick speaking again.

"I do not think we shall wait any longer. Instead, we shall proceed to the library – but not to dance or any such thing! No indeed, there shall be *many* a game at this house party! Yes, we are to be provided with a great deal of entertainment during your time here, but on occasion we shall be required to make our own entertainment... as we shall do this evening."

Chuckling good naturedly, Rebecca grinned as Miss Moir looped her arm through hers so they might walk together. It appeared this was to be the beginning of a most excellent holiday.

"Do you know who it is that is yet to arrive?" Rebecca asked quietly, as Lady Meyrick spoke quietly to her son, who had interrupted her for some reason.

"No, I do not know," Miss Moir shot her a glance. "But I, myself, would not *dare* to be tardy to something such as this, not when the Duke and his mother have shown such generosity!"

Rebecca shrugged. "Mayhap those still absent are well known to the Duke and had always stated they would be tardy?"

"Mayhap," Miss Moir looked around the room at each guest in turn as they waited to make their way to the library. "I admit I am eager to know who else is to arrive!"

"As am I." Rebecca grinned at her friend just as Lady Meyrick clapped her hands brightly, catching everyone's attention again. The bright smile on the lady's face reflected the joy and anticipation in Rebecca's heart as she waited to hear what it was they were to do.

"We shall begin by playing ourselves a few hands of cards. However, it shall be a little different, for there will be forfeits for those who lose, but gifts for the winner!"

This was met by murmurs of excitement as Rebecca's heart skipped a beat in a thrill of anticipation. She was already looking forward to the game, wondering whether she would have any chance of winning, and if she did, what the gift she would receive might be. A million ideas went through her mind as she battled to catch her breath. There was often a good deal less consideration to propriety and society's customs at such occasions, according to her mother. They were a good deal freer, no longer bound by a set of strict and rigid rules. This was a chance to laugh, to make merry and to enjoy every moment of being here. She was already looking forward to it.

"If you would like to make your way through to the library, the card tables have already been set out."

Unwilling to show any great eagerness for fear of being teased about it by either her mother or her friend, Rebecca stood quietly but did not move.

"Come!" Miss Moir immediately moved forward, tugging Rebecca along with her. "What do you suppose the forfeits might be?"

Rebecca laughed as they made to quit of the room. "I confess I can think of a great many things, but I cannot be certain whether I am correct!"

Miss Moir bit her lip. "I do hope I shall not fail. I would be most embarrassed should I make a fool of myself."

Rebecca pressed her friend's hand. "I do not think you need to have any fear in that regard, my dear friend. The forfeits will not be severe. They may make us a little embarrassed, but it is all in good humor. At least, that is what my mother has told me!"

At this, Miss Moir let out a long breath. "I understand. There will be nothing of any severity."

"Nothing." Rebecca smiled as she walked into the library. "Absolutely. In fact, I do believe there will be nothing in all the time we reside here that should bring you any shame, embarrassment, upset, or anger."

With a smile still upon her face, she walked directly into the room, only to come to a sudden halt. To her utter horror, she perceived a gentleman standing directly opposite her, a gentleman whom she recognized immediately but whom she had vowed never to see again. Her breath hitched as she looked directly at him.

Surely it could not be. Fate would not be so cruel to demand this of her, would not take such a happy occasion and quite ruin it by his presence, would it? And yet, it appeared she was to have such misfortune, for the one gentleman sitting there was the one who had broken her heart. The gentleman who had taken all from her, who had left her with nothing – and at the end, begged her to keep it from the ears and eyes of the *ton*. A gentleman who now went pale as he realized who she was, a shadow in his eyes as he looked at her.

And everything suddenly went very cold indeed.

OH, no! It seems someone from her past was invited to the house party...someone she didn't want to see again! Check out the rest of the story in the Kindle store The Lady's Christmas Kiss